BULLETS IN
THE SUN

BULLETS IN THE SUN

A Western Story

ROBERT J. HORTON

Skyhorse Publishing

First Skyhorse Publishing edition published 2015 by arrangement with Golden West Literary Agency

Copyright © 2011 by Golden West Literary Agency

"Bullets in the Sun" first appeared as a six-part serial in Street and Smith's *Western Story Magazine* (3/8/31-5/2/31). Copyright © 1931 by Street & Smith Publications, Inc. Copyright © renewed 1959 by Street & Smith Publications, Inc. Acknowledgment is made to Condé Nast Publications, Inc., for their co-operation. Copyright © 2011 by Golden West Literary Agency for restored material.

Skyhorse Publishing books may be purchased in bulk at special discounts for sales promotion, corporate gifts, fund-raising, or educational purposes. Special editions can also be created to specifications. For details, contact the Special Sales Department, Skyhorse Publishing, 307 West 36th Street, 11th Floor, New York, NY 10018 or info@skyhorsepublishing.com.

Skyhorse® and Skyhorse Publishing® are registered trademarks of Skyhorse Publishing, Inc.®, a Delaware corporation.

Visit our website at www.skyhorsepublishing.com.

10 9 8 7 6 5 4 3 2 1

Library of Congress Cataloging-in-Publication Data is available on file.

Cover design by Brian Peterson

Print ISBN: 978-1-62087-824-8
Ebook ISBN: 978-1-62914-893-9

Printed in the United States of America

Chapter One

For a wicked town, Sunrise had the sweetest name and the most ideal location of any cluster of weather-beaten false fronts and board shacks in the Crazy Butte country, which meant the east Teton range. It was as if some evil genius had set it down, ready-made, in its idyllic setting, as a lure—a trap for the unwary who would find its enticing beauty a mirage.

Between the resorts and other buildings that lined its short main street grew towering cottonwoods, whose graceful branches arched and weaved and purred in the wandering winds. A stream, crystal-clear, meandered through it, its banks green and sprinkled with nodding willows. And on all sides the plains rolled away in waves of gold to splash in purple breakers against the hills. Over all this, ten miles to eastward, Crazy Butte reared its rose-and-turquoise crown.

It was as though Nature strove to draw a veil of camouflage about the town's rough exterior. For Sunrise was notoriously bad, outrageously wicked, reckless, and as wide open as the arching blue vault of the sky.

And if an evil genius had seen fit so to place the town, then that genius also had chosen to put Big Tom Lester at the head of it. In Sunrise, Tom Lester's word was the only approach to law. His was the largest resort, the Red Arrow, and he dominated most of the others. He boasted acquaintance with every outlaw, cut-throat, killer, rustler, gambler, and tinhorn in the vast Crazy Butte district. He possessed a flaming tongue and wore a ready gun. It was said he had his clutching fingers deep in the spoils of every

1

band operating north of the Teton River. Men who could beat him to the draw he bent to his will by the sheer ferocious force of his personality. He was as big physically as he was powerful otherwise, black-eyed, with ruddy veins tracing intricate patterns on his cruel face, thick-lipped, square-jawed, aggressive, malignant.

At some time or other, sooner or later, every shady character that came into the Crazy Butte region drifted to Sunrise and into the Red Arrow to report. The resort boasted the longest bar north of the Missouri, drink of volcanic strength, every conceivable gaming device, a dance floor and women to keep it busy, limitless poker, and any kind of a welcome a newcomer might desire. Forty feuds had been shot out in the street in front of it and in the space between its near wall and the corrals behind it. The Red Arrow, then, was the hot spot in the wildest town between the Missouri and the line.

On this warm May night, Sunrise was thronged with the first big influx of visitors after the tardy retreat of winter from the north ranges.

Big Tom stood at the lower end of his long bar, a black cigar thrust between his thick lips, his pudgy fingers beating a tattoo on the surface before him. The bar was lined three deep. Card tables were filling and other games drawing a patronage that indicated capacity business by midnight. Big Tom's eyes gleamed with a fierce light of exultation. This was his kingdom.

A slight, wasp-like man, tanned and wrinkled, beady-eyed, glided through the throng, twisting and sidling like a snake until he reached Big Tom Lester's side. He hardly came up to the big man's shoulder, and Lester did not look down at him but inclined his head.

"Mills is in town," said the small man in a voice that barely carried to Big Tom's ear.

The Red Arrow proprietor showed no flash of interest. But he now looked down into the other's eyes. "Where?" he asked. "Who's with him?"

"Just put up his horse," replied the small man. "He's alone. Must have rode clear in from Milton, way he looked. Dust, an' sweat, an' . . ."

"Go keep an eye on him, Porky," the larger man commanded. "He'll be comin' to see me. Keep this to yourself an' I don't want him bothered."

When the wasp-like figure slipped away, Big Tom motioned to a bartender who quickly served him a drink. He toyed with his glass, his eyes slightly narrowed, a thin furrow of thought showing above his bushy brows. Then he tossed off the libation and waited. After a time he raised his empty glass a few inches from the bar and put it down.

A man at the upper end of the long counter detached himself from some companions and made his way leisurely down to Big Tom's station. This man was dressed after the manner of a fancier of the gaming tables. He was dark and handsome, smooth-shaven, with flashing brown eyes, and a smooth, satiny skin. Diamonds flashed about him. When he arrived at Big Tom's side, he crooked a finger at the man in the white coat nearest them as a signal for a drink.

"Porky tells me Mills is in town," said Big Tom in his ordinary voice. "Do you know anything?"

"Not a thing," said the other. "Nothing big has been pulled this spring, so far."

Big Tom scowled. "Well, Farlin, there's something behind it, you can lay to that. An' this is the first time he ever came out here alone. *That* means something."

Farlin pursed his lips. He put a hand above his right ear where the hair was gray. "Alone, eh? I don't believe it."

"Porky's word is pretty good," said Big Tom curtly. "But why . . . that's what I would like to know."

"Here's one that can't tell you," said Farlin coolly. "I've never seen anything sensible about the law yet."

"That's all right to say in Sunrise." Big Tom frowned. "But Mills isn't such a fool. If Porky says he's alone, he is alone, an' it takes something besides nerve to drag Mills here by his lonesome."

Farlin rolled a brown-paper cigarette with white, tapering fingers, steady as steel. "Overconfidence," he suggested, sliding the edge of the paper along his tongue.

"Mills ain't that kind," growled Big Tom Lester.

"Then he has some men cached around here somewhere," Farlin decided, touching the flame to his smoke.

"What good would that do him?" asked Lester crossly.

"That's just it." Farlin nodded. "An' what good would it do him to try to bring a bunch of men in here? He's got too much sense to attempt that. He's safer without 'em."

A second line traced a seam across Big Tom's forehead. "It seems that way," he conceded. "Pass the word around that I don't want him noticed if he comes in here, an' he's pretty sure to come here before the night's over."

"I'll do that," said Farlin. "Is Porky trailing him?"

"Porky's outside," was the reply. "He'll likely slip me a sign. Better stir along. I reckon everybody here doesn't know him."

"But plenty do," was Farlin's soft rejoinder as he moved away.

* * * * *

An hour later Big Tom started as a tall figure loomed at his side.

"'Evening, Tom," said a cool, drawling voice. "Warm for May."

The resort proprietor turned his head and surveyed the speaker coldly. "Safer to come in the front way, Mills," he said crisply.

"Shorter by the back," said Sheriff Mills. "And your man Porky didn't have a chance to sneak a signal. You know, Tom, sometimes I think Porky ain't so smart."

"What'll you have to drink?" asked Big Tom with a scowl.

"Same as yourself," drawled the official. "I wouldn't risk the common stock, Tom."

Lester bit his lip and signaled the bartender. "Now," he said, when they had been served, "let's have it down the alley."

"You mean the drink." Mills smiled, raising his glass. "We'll talk in your office."

The sheriff had been the cynosure of stealthy eyes. By this time every man in town that knew him knew he was there. But none stared at him directly. The two finished their drinks and turned into Big Tom's private office behind the end of the bar.

The resort proprietor proffered cigars and Mills accepted one without hesitation. "Tom, you know how to pick good whiskey, good cigars, an' good locations," he said as he lit the weed and blew a fragrant ring of smoke aloft.

"You ought to be glad I can pick the last," said Lester dryly.

"It shows you have judgment, anyway," was Mills's comment.

"I don't bother you none out here," Lester snapped.

"Not directly," Mills drawled. "Not directly, Tom. And you've got a good crowd for so early."

"It's a long time since you've been out this way," said the other. "I don't reckon you just come for the ride."

Mills shook his head. "I'm getting too old to ride for pleasure, Tom. Any of the big boys up north yet?"

Big Tom's eyes slowly narrowed. "If there's one thing you didn't ride out here for, it's to get information," he said darkly. "You know me better than that."

"Oh, I have had information," said Mills, waving his cigar. "But them it concerned should have known better than to cross Big Tom Lester. You're not above that sort of thing, Tom."

Lester's eyes were glittering, and he bit the sharp answer from his tongue. "They're all big fellows here, one way or another," he managed to get out.

"They are," Mills nodded. "I agree with you. And taken together they make up the biggest bunch of cut-throats between here and doomsday."

Big Tom met his gaze steadily. "We'll let that go as it stands," he said with a faint smile in which there lingered no trace of mirth.

"As I knew it would," said Mills sternly. "Now, Tom, there's a big fellow on his way up here you haven't met. You won't like him, because he won't be afraid of you. If you call him, he'll just naturally tell you to go to blazes . . . maybe give you a ticket, and send that mean little gunfighter of a Porky along with you. Now, I see you're interested. Who wants the information now?"

Lester's face went white, then black, then white again. "You're . . . you're takin' a big chance, Mills," he rasped. "What're you doin' it for?"

"I'm not taking a chance in the world," replied the sheriff coldly. "I'd be taking a chance, maybe, if I rode in here with a force of men. But, alone, I have you to protect me. Don't think I came here without certain parties knowing my destination. You couldn't kill me and get away with it, and you know it. I'm just wearing' a gun because it's part of my equipment."

Lester half rose, and then sat down hard in his chair by the desk.

"I'll bite," he shot through his teeth. "Who's this big one you're spoutin' about?"

"I thought so," said Mills with evident satisfaction. "The gent's name is Bovert. Ever hear of him?"

Big Tom had gripped the arms of his chair. His eyes popped. "Not up here!" he ejaculated, incredulous.

"Why not?" Sheriff Mills raised his brows. "There are soft pickings to be had here, are there not? Isn't this a loose town? Isn't this a wide-open joint? Don't you welcome visitors who are . . . ?"

Lester interrupted with an oath. "If Bovert comes here," he snarled, "if he comes here . . ."

"You'll gather him in, if you can," Mills put in mildly. "He's bad medicine, Tom. He can shoot a bullet in the air and split it with a second shot. He's got hair on his head and brains inside it. You'll surely be nice to him, I reckon."

Lester made no reply to this. Then: "Why did you come here to tell me he was comin'?" he asked, his face dark with suspicion.

"Bovert is no friend of mine," said Mills. "I couldn't send word, so I had to come myself. I want to ask you to lay off him when he comes. Now, don't ask me why. I want your promise to let him alone, unless . . . no, I want your promise to let him strictly alone. Do I get it?"

Big Tom stared. "You want him whitewashed?" he gasped. "Why, he's worse than any of the crowd here."

"That's why I want him left alone," said Mills evenly. He surveyed the other under knitted brows. "I don't know as I ever asked anything of you before," he said slowly. "If I ever did, I've forgotten it. It's out of the way over here, and they can't hear the echoes in the county seat. Not that I'd be scared about my job," he added hastily, "for this county can have my badge any time it wants it. I've bothered you some, and maybe I'll bother you again. I don't figure I'll be under any obligations in return for this favor. But I guess you'll understand that we . . . that I'll appreciate it."

"Oh . . . ." Big Tom waved a hand in a generous gesture. "We understand each other. How'd you find out Bovert was headed north?"

"The meadowlarks brought the word," said Mills dryly. "Do I get the promise? It ought to puff you up to see that I'm willing to take your word."

"I've been known to keep it," Big Tom snapped. "You should tell me more so I . . ."

Mills had risen from his chair. "Do I get it?" he demanded sharply.

"Suppose I can't stop . . . anything?" Lester evaded.

"That'll be hard luck," said Sheriff Mills grimly. "For the last time, Tom, do I get it?"

"Yes, you have it," snarled Big Tom Lester savagely.

They went out and drank amicably at the bar.

"Tell Porky my horse is branded," drawled Mills as he left and walked the length of the room and out the front entrance, leaving the Red Arrow proprietor glaring at the wasp-like gunman who was now waiting for orders.

Chapter Two

None ever would have suspected that Dan Farlin was fifty-five years old, as he admitted; anyone would have been astounded to learn that he was nearly sixty. Straight of bearing, perfect in poise, smooth, clear complexion, dark-haired except where a becoming gray showed over his temples, suave, urbane, polished—he was the closest approach to a gentleman on the whole north range. Always he dressed in a dark, double-breasted suit, with a soft gray shirt of silk and wool, a blue four-in-hand in which sparkled a two-carat diamond, blue-white, deep, and flawless. A soft gray hat, and black-buttoned shoes, with gray silk socks, completed his attire. He wore a four-carat diamond on the middle finger of his left hand and he would not have been Dan Farlin without it. He was generous to a fault, inexorable as an opponent at cards, accomplished in the many ways of the professional gambler and the man who lives splendidly by his wits.

He was the one man Big Tom Lester respected, the one man in whose presence the lord of Sunrise felt vaguely uneasy, the one man who could disconcert him merely by a look. Which is doubtless why Dan Farlin was closeted with Big Tom in the latter's private office a few minutes after Sheriff Mills had taken his departure.

"Do you believe he came here to tell me Bovert was headed this way?" asked Lester in a worried voice.

"Why not?" said Farlin, arching his brows. "Mills is one of the old school and doesn't lie. I told you he would be safer if he came alone, and he told you the same thing. He told you he couldn't send a messenger, so you say, and he couldn't. As far as I can make out, from what you have told me, he came here on exactly the mission he explained. I don't blame you for feeling suspicious, however."

Big Tom leaned forward with his hands on his knees. "Do you know much about this Bovert, Dan?" he asked. "You were south last winter, an' you get around more than I do. I didn't want to show my . . . my ignorance to Mills, but I don't even know what this Bovert looks like."

"Nor do I," said Farlin, building a cigarette. "Yes, I've heard of him. He's a lone worker and a fast one. He goes in for big stuff. His reputation down in the desert country is young, but he may have worked somewhere else before under another name. Tell the truth, I wasn't much interested. I was merely putting in the winter down there, playing a little cards, taking the waters at the springs, giving Gladys a chance for a little more schooling and music in San Antone . . . buying a hundred-thousand-dollar ranch." He lit his cigarette with a graceful gesture.

"You what!" Big Tom gasped out. "Buyin' a . . . a hundred-thousand-dollar ranch! A . . . ranch?"

Dan Farlin laughed softly, musically. His gaze was quizzical as he looked at Lester.

"My dear Tom," he said with a delightful suggestion of drawl, "you don't think this is going to last forever, do you? Sooner or later the works are going to blow up. The explosion is coming suddenly, when it does come. There'll be no time fuse. I've been through this sort of play before. I'm not so young. I'm old enough so that when it comes this time, I'm not going to be caught with a saddle and no horse. But don't let what I'm saying worry you. I don't expect it will, and I don't want it to. But I've got Gladys to think of. You see I'm not alone, this time."

"That girl?" Big Tom frowned.

"We'll leave her out of it," said Farlin sharply.

Big Tom Lester shifted uneasily in his chair. Whenever Farlin spoke and looked at him like that, it nonplussed him, and such was Farlin's attitude whenever Lester spoke of the gambler's daughter, Gladys—the fair flower that bloomed in that questionable garden of guarded misdeeds and strife.

"Well, now, Dan," the resort proprietor resumed briskly, "I'm wonderin' . . . since we don't know what this bad *hombre* looks like . . . how will we know him when he gets here?"

Farlin chuckled. "In the first place, Tom, he'll be a stranger. We get lots of strangers, but Bovert should turn out to be a different brand of stranger. You know men pretty well, and I have met pretty near all kinds. I guess we'll be able . . . between the two of us . . . to make him out by his looks, his actions, or his general manner. And there's always a chance that some of the crowd may have met up with him before."

"That's so," said Lester, brightening. "Still, I don't want it to get noised about that a bad one's coming. An', confound that Mills, I promised to let him alone. If some of the boys get wise to him, they might pick a fight just to put him under. Then Mills would blame me, although I can't see what he could do about it, even if he did."

"Mills is half bluffing," said Farlin, frowning. "Not all bluff, understand. He knows he couldn't do anything but rout us out, if he could do that. But he's got me interested, for one, and I'm for laying off this Bovert and trying to find out why Mills wants him protected." He paused and stared at the end of his cigarette. "There's a chance we might get something on Mills," he said softly. "Did you ever think of that, Tom?"

Lester's eyes widened. "Snakes, yes!" he exclaimed. "You know, I haven't always pegged you for the smartest man in Sunrise for nothing, Dan." He beamed.

"Except yourself," Farlin observed dryly.

Lester's smile vanished. It irritated him that he never had been able to compliment this man, as he could others of his followers possessed of lesser intellects. For Farlin was immune to flattery. To praise him for anything was futile.

"There's another matter, Dan," he said, changing the subject. "It seems to me that during the last year or so Porky's brain has been drying up."

"He had one, then?" Farlin inquired mildly.

"I never asked him to think for me," Lester snapped out in a heat. "Lately I suspect him of gettin' nosey."

Farlin smiled. "That wouldn't be healthy, so far as you are concerned, would it?" he asked pleasantly.

Lester frowned darkly. "He's useful in a good many ways," he confessed. "But I'm afraid he'll forget where his usefulness ends."

"I'm not interested in that," said Farlin. "Tell me . . . did Mills want to know when this Bovert arrives? That is, did he ask you to send him word, or anything?"

Big Tom shook his head. "Nope. I told Porky to tell me if he left town, an' as Porky ain't back he must have stayed over. Maybe he figures to see me again before he leaves."

"I doubt it," said Farlin, "but you never can tell about the law. It works like a merry-go-round, its wonders to perform. If this is all, Tom, I'll go out and take my evening's nourishment of stud. I'm just laying low till Lawson and his crowd come in with a stake. They're due pretty quick now from that bank job . . . if they made it."

"No danger of Lawson fallin' down," Big Tom grunted. "He'll be back with plenty. I only hope he doesn't bring a couple of posses trailin' him."

Farlin laughed. "To hear you talk, one would think you were losing your nerve," was his parting rejoinder.

It might have been said in the spirit of banter, but it left Big Tom Lester slumped in his chair, an unlighted cigar in his mouth, a thoughtful look in his cruel eyes. Dan Farlin was too smart!

* * * * *

Dan Farlin stood at the lower end of the bar, tall and handsome, his soft gray hat pulled over his eyes, shading them from the yellow beams that slanted through the smoke layers from the hanging lamps. He was the personification of ease and elegance, and he was listening to a slip of a girl with a rose-white face, wide, dark eyes, and an abundance of auburn hair, who was singing. She had the soft, sweet voice of her mother, who had thus sung before her, who Dan Farlin had married, who had left him this daughter. Three times each night she sang, and, at such times, the clamor of the busy resort was stilled, and the men removed their hats. It was good business, thought Big Tom; it gave the girl something to do, thought Handsome Dan.

The song ended, the room burst into prolonged applause.

"That's the ticket, little one!" A tall celebrant, evidently just off the range, pushed forward and held out a handful of gold. "Here's for the song, an' there's another basketful for a kiss!"

The applause suddenly was stilled. The girl struck the hand, and the gold pieces rang on the floor. Then the girl's palm came smartly across the cowpuncher's mouth.

A cheer swelled from two hundred throats.

Dan Farlin leaped just as the bold one stepped toward the girl. He caught the man by the arm and whirled him about.

"Get out!" he commanded sharply. "Get out or I'll drag you into the street and rinse out your mouth with dust!"

The other sneered. "Who're you, anyway, you . . . ."

That was all. Farlin's right drove the man's speech into his throat and he dropped on his haunches on the edge of the low platform.

"That was my card," said Farlin. "Are you going? Or do you want the address?"

Several bystanders grasped the man and hustled him out the rear way. Gladys Farlin, the roses faded from her cheeks, stood holding a tiny, pearl-handled revolver in her hand, looking at her father.

"Come with me," she said through lips trembling with anger.

In the little dressing room behind the dance floor she turned on him. "Why did you do it?" she demanded, stamping her foot angrily. "Why did you do it?"

"You didn't think I was going to watch it, did you?" said her father, frowning. "And hereafter you're not to carry that gun."

"I suppose not," said the girl scornfully. "I expect my big, strong daddy will always be around as bouncer to make a fool of me. Is that it?"

"It's only the second time such a thing has happened," said Dan Farlin sternly. "and I just chanced to be there. Any man in the place would protect you from insult, and you know it. You . . . might kill somebody with that pistol. Ever think of that?"

"If I have to shoot it, somebody will get hurt, at least," was the answer. "You say this has happened twice. There's always a third time and out." She dropped into an easy chair, putting the gun inside her dress.

"I think you will have to give this up," said Dan Farlin, his face gray. "I've had that idea for some time." He could not say that he altogether understood this wild spirit before him.

"Yes?" said Gladys languidly. "Well, it's an idea you might as well get out of your head. It's empty . . . the idea, I mean."

"You . . . you like this?" her father faltered. Was her mother's blood running riot in this offspring?

"Of course I don't like it," was the ready answer. "But it's all I have, isn't it?"

"You could stay south," he pointed out. "I've told you that before." Even as he said it, he experienced a guilty thrill of apprehension. He was selfish in wanting to have the girl near him.

"Not unless you stay there, Daddy," she said flippantly. "I won't leave you up here alone, and I won't stop singing here, because I want to keep an eye on you. Now, you have two reasons to puncture your idea balloon."

Farlin stared at her. "You never put it that way before," he blurted. Some of his poise had fled.

"When I did put it, I put it straight," she retorted with a toss of her lovely head. Then her eyes clouded. "Oh, Daddy, I don't see why we both can't go south and live there the rest of our lives. In the sun, with the scent of mesquite burning, with the warm desert winds, with guitars strumming, and the pepper trees waving in the breeze. There's music in the south, Daddy, and here . . ." She stopped short, biting a trembling lip.

"Yes, yes," he prompted hurriedly. "Go on."

"There's something else, Daddy," she said softly. "I want young people. I'm nineteen, Daddy, and there are only two or three girls I can associate with here, and no boys."

No boys! Farlin's heart missed a beat. "You're too young to be thinking about boys, Gladys," he stammered.

"Would you like to have one come along . . . here?" she asked quietly.

"You don't know what you're talking about," her father said angrily. "Just get such ideas out of your head. I've gone in pretty deep down there, as you know. I need this season up here. Maybe next season."

"There it is," she interrupted. "Maybe next season. It's always next season. You've been saying that for years. And next season it will be the same, and the next . . . if you have your way."

"But, Gladys, I haven't wanted you to come back up here with me for the last three years," he protested. He knew he lied.

"I've got to come, Daddy. I couldn't let you come back here alone. Don't you think I remember when I was a little girl and mother was alive . . . how she used to worry when you were gone? I was born in this country, Daddy. I know that you are always in danger. I know you have to have some restraining influence, and that's what I am. Without me here, you'd take chances you wouldn't take with me around. You know it very well. And, what's more, you know you really want me here."

Dan Farlin was silent for a space. "I guess I'm selfish," he said finally, "but you're all I have."

"And what would I do if you were gone? You have money enough, Daddy. Why, I've got quite a lot of money myself. And we don't have to keep that old ranch, pretty as it is. We have enough, if you'd only think so."

"I've got to have just one more season," Farlin said stoutly. "I promise you, Gladys . . . and don't tell a soul . . . that next year we won't come back."

"But anything can happen this year, Daddy," said the girl, rising and putting her arms about his neck. "There's . . . there's always the danger. You can put it off a season, a month . . . even a day . . . and it might be too late. Why can't we go now?"

"Because . . . there's a reason why it is impossible," said Dan Farlin coldly, sternly. "You'll have to accept that explanation. Now, dearie, be good. And promise me you won't sing again tonight."

"Oh, that's easy," she said, turning away in resignation. "I won't sing for your sake, because you're worried about something. But I'm not afraid for myself."

* * * * *

At the upper end of the bar Big Tom Lester greeted Farlin with a smile. "Better get that look off your face, Dan. Lawson's crowd just rode in."

Chapter Three

Now Dan Farlin looked down the bar to where a towering figure loomed above the crowd. This was Ed Lawson, jovial but deadly outlaw, leader of a band of desperadoes that ranged far from the Crazy Butte country in carrying out their depredations. Lawson had made it a point not to disturb this district, where he virtually found sanctuary between raids. When he next left with his band, he might be gone for days, weeks, or months; he might not return that season. His men were sure pickings for Dan Farlin. It would be the gambler's first respectable haul of the season just starting.

"Does Lawson know Mills is in town?" Farlin asked Big Tom.

"Not only knows he's here, but knows he's alone," replied Lester. "One of his men trailed him in. You know, Lawson isn't afraid of Mills. This is the closest he ever goes to Rocky Point."

Farlin nodded. Rocky Point was the county seat. It was a sizable town, a shipping point for cattle and banking and supply headquarters for all that section. It was fed, too, by the mines in the Little Rockies. Incidentally Rocky Point supplied Sunrise with considerable business of a doubtful but profitable nature.

Lawson's heavy voice boomed above the tumult, ordering refreshments for the house. He soon would delegate this phase of his visit to henchmen and take a turn at the cards. At his side was Red Cole, his right bower, and a gunfighter second only to himself. Lawson forbade his men to fight in town, and his order was generally carried out.

"Shows sign of being heavy," Farlin commented.

"He's carryin' plenty," said Big Tom with an eager note in his voice. "An' his crowd is heavy, too. I don't know where they turned the trick, but it was juicy."

"West," snorted Farlin. "Sheepshearing money, likely. I always feel like a common thief, playing with that gang."

Big Tom flashed him a queer look. The incident of the unruly cowpuncher and the girl had disturbed him. But it wasn't like Farlin to show it when he was disturbed. The resort proprietor laid it to the start of the season.

"You've got to get your hand in," he said in a smooth voice. "You couldn't ask for better material to practice on."

Farlin glanced at him coldly. "You know, Lester, I don't cheat at cards . . . except to stop the other fellow from cheating. But you've never believed that."

"I only know you get the money an' give me a decent split for workin' here," said Lester irritably. "An' that's enough for me."

"Suppose I was to stop giving you a split," said Farlin softly. "Ever think of that?"

Big Tom stared at him as if he couldn't believe his ears.

"Think it over and remember to keep in good humor when you're talking to me," said Farlin coldly. He walked away in the direction of a roulette wheel to play idly and await the call from Lawson that was sure to come.

For the second time that night, Big Tom Lester found himself somewhat bewildered, thinking deeply and to no purpose, as a result of a remark made by the gambler. What the devil! Here was the sheriff in town, a notorious outlaw present, and Farlin showing a queer streak of rebellion against his lot—and the formidable specter of the unknown Bovert in the background. Sunrise was getting off to a fast start this spring.

* * * * *

There was a full table of seven in the stud poker game in a private room in the rear of the Red Arrow that night. Farlin was in the slot running the game for the house. But his sole duty consisted in seeing that the house received its percentage of the play according to the size of the pots. He played his cards entirely on his own and wagered his own money. But he did not have to deduct a percentage from the stakes he won unless he chose to do so.

Ed Lawson, big, dark-faced, with black eyes and mustache—a powerful man of great physique with hairy hands—dominated the game. There was none of the silent, calculating gambler about him. He played recklessly and shoved large sums into the center of the table in efforts to draw cards to match his hand or beat another's. He talked incessantly, and Dan Farlin, cool and accomplished, hated him for this trait and despised him generally. Red Cole played a tight game, a perpetual frown wrinkling his brow; he showed his small, white teeth in a mean smile when he lost, to conceal his chagrin. He was a hard loser. The other four were members of Lawson's outfit, men who cared little for money or the future. Woodenheads, Farlin called them. There were no spectators.

"I've a mind to send word to the sheriff an' ask him to set in," boomed Lawson. "I guess one of the boys would give him his seat." He laughed uproariously.

"I wouldn't do it," said Farlin quietly.

"I won't." Lawson chuckled. "I won't bother him so long as he don't bother me. A hundred, Farlin? Another ace in the hole, eh? You may be a smart gambler, Dan, but here's one *hombre* that can read you like a book. Raise it two hundred, my seven of diamonds in sight against your king. Let's play cards."

Farlin met the raise and bit his lip in vexation. Of all the men he played with, Lawson came nearest to disturbing his outward calm and causing him to overplay his cards. He had to watch himself in this game. It galled him to think that he had to depend on Lawson's loot for his season's start. He needed money. He had gone in far deeper there in the south than he had let Gladys or

Big Tom suspect. When he had told his daughter it was impossible for him to quit, he had told the truth. He was chained to the tables until Christmas, and it might come to a point where he would have to use more than ordinary skill. He flipped Ed Lawson a second seven in sight, took a jack for himself, and raised the outlaw's bet $500 without change of expression.

"Just what I told you!" bawled Lawson. "Playin' a lucky ace! Sevens for luck, an' what's five hundred iron men? If I had to work for 'em as hard as you do, Dan, I'd play 'em close to my watch chain. Five hundred more that I've got your goat. Let's play cards."

Farlin had winced at this speech. Now his face went a shade whiter.

"It'll take more than one raid to get my goat, Lawson," he said in a cool, pleasant voice. His smile was genuine. "And if I make my money hard, I don't take the chances you do."

"Sometimes I think you ain't got the nerve," growled Lawson.

Red Cole laughed and the look he shot Farlin was one of contempt. The others were interested. This was the nearest approach to a tilt they ever had seen between Farlin and the outlaw leader.

Farlin calmly dealt Lawson a third seven and dropped a second king for himself. Lawson flushed and gazed keenly at the gambler for several seconds.

"I pass," he said.

"A thousand," said Farlin. "We're playing cards, Ed."

Lawson called the bet. On the next deal he drew a nine and Farlin drew the fourth seven. A gasp went up from the others who had dropped out.

Lawson stared. "I'll call one bet," he said.

"Then I'll make it easy," said Farlin, "and call it another thousand."

He turned his hole card to display the third king.

Lawson laughed and looked at his watch. "I'll play till daylight an' no longer," he announced. He took a thick roll of yellow-backed bills from a side pocket of his coat. "I'll make you work to get it," he said, looking steadily at Farlin.

The gambler smiled faintly. "That's what I'm here for, Ed, to get it."

"Are we all in this game or just you two?" Cole demanded.

"You'll get service for your money," said Farlin coldly.

"I don't like this game," Cole snapped out.

"I guess we can find a customer to take your place if you don't feel satisfied," said Farlin, while Lawson looked from one to the other of them in amusement.

"It ain't what I feel, it's what I know!" blurted Cole.

"Shut up!" Lawson commanded. "Never flirt with a Derringer in an old-time gambler's cuff." He laughed in Farlin's face and struck the table with the palm of his hand.

Cole kicked back his chair and leaped to his feet. "I'm quittin'!" he cried. "I'm through keepin' a pussy-foot cardsharp in clean clothes an' strawberries. If he can deal a Derringer as good as he can deal cards, I'm givin' him the chance."

Lawson's manner had changed on the instant. His eyes were glittering orbs of ice. "Beat it, Red," he said sternly. "Outside!"

Cole wavered in his glances. But his slight form was tense. Then he turned to the door with a nod to the others.

"And stay there," Farlin shot after him as he went out.

Lawson tore up his cards with a harsh laugh. "A new deck," he ordered. "Let's play cards!"

Dawn filtered through the cracks in the green shade on the single window at last. The chair Cole had vacated remained unoccupied. Farlin suspected that Cole had seen to it that no other customer applied. Half of Lawson's big bank roll was gone. Dan Farlin was the heavy winner. He pocketed his winnings listlessly after Lawson had looked at his watch and called off the game.

"We're not stayin' in town long this trip," he told the gambler, "an' I don't want the men roaming around for Mills to look at."

When they left the room, the outlaw turned to Farlin. "Let's have breakfast together," he suggested. "I want to talk to you."

Farlin hesitated. "I usually go home for breakfast . . . ."

"I know, I know," said Lawson impatiently. "That girl of yours will be expectin' you, maybe. But she knows I'm in town an' she wouldn't be surprised if you stayed for a long session. We'll step up to the Crazy Café an' take one of them booths."

When they were in the booth and the waiter had drawn the curtains after taking their order, Lawson lost no time in getting down to business.

"Cole was wise," he said with a significant nod. "I don't want you an' Cole to have any trouble. I'll tell him quick today."

"I don't think either of you are as wise as you think," was Farlin's cool comment.

Lawson's eyes narrowed. "It wasn't a square deal, Dan," he said slowly. "An' it was, so far as I know, the first time you pulled a trick on me. You know how I gamble, an' you know you don't have to deal queer to take me. I'm tellin' you straight that I'd rather have you win from me at cards than any man I know. I always expect you to win from me." He paused to let the words sink in, while Farlin gazed at him out of eyes that were expressionless.

"You might say I'm one of your charities," said Farlin.

"An' I wouldn't be far from right." Lawson nodded. "But I saw more tonight than you thought, Dan. You're out to make a clean-up this year. You want the money, an' you intend to get it. I don't blame you a bit. I can see the handwriting on the wall, old-timer. You intend to shake Sunrise, an' I don't blame you for that, either. I wouldn't hint anything to Big Tom . . . he's a fool, anyway . . . but watch him. He isn't ready to quit."

"How about yourself?" asked Farlin quietly.

Lawson compressed his lips. "This territory is gettin' to be worked out," he said grimly. "If you was to repeat that, it would mean trouble for me. So I'm trusting you. Dan, why in thunder should you slave all summer an' fall an' right up into the blizzards for a stake from the tables when there's another way . . . a short cut to a bigger stake in less time an' with less trouble." He tapped the table with the fingers of his right hand.

"That's easy to answer," replied Farlin with a frown. "I'm not alone in the world. The short cut you talk about might be altogether too short. And besides I'm not experienced in that sort of play."

"What sort of play?" asked Lawson. "You don't know what I'm gettin' at a-tall. Do you think I want you to get on a horse an' join us in a raid? You couldn't do it even if you wanted to. For one thing, you're too soft. Twenty miles of hard ridin' would lay you up for a week. You're well-preserved an' healthy, an', if you drift along quiet, you'll live a long time. It takes money to live, Dan, to live like you want to live. Also, for fast shootin' an' a quick getaway, you'd be a total loss. But in another an' easier way, you'd be the clear, sugar-coated candy with chocolate trimmin's."

"Sounds interesting," Farlin observed. "Do I understand that you have some kind of a proposition up your sleeve?"

"I'm comin' to that," Lawson answered. "But I've got to know that you won't let our little talk go any farther than this booth."

"That's understood," said Farlin. "I've listened and forgotten before this. I'm not in your game, and you know it, but most naturally I'm a bit curious."

"That's enough. Dan, I've worked around this district for a long time, but always *away* from it. An' all this time I've left a plant, side-stepped as sweet a job as a man followin' the trail I'm on could want. But it isn't a ride-in, stick-'em-up, shoot-it-off, an' ride-out lay. This job has to be pulled with more . . . what is it? . . . more . . ?"

"Finesse," Farlin supplied with a thin smile.

"That's it," Lawson agreed. "An' that's where you would fit in so sweet. Now, do you begin to get my drift?"

Farlin was toying with a fork, studying the tablecloth, his brow furrowed. He looked older. Suddenly he glanced up and spoke almost in a whisper. "Rocky Point?" He dropped the fork as Lawson nodded silently.

"Big game," said the gambler.

"An' big stakes," said Lawson in a low voice. "Dan, there's never been a word said, but Mills don't expect me to go anywhere near that town, an' he don't expect any of my men to go anywhere near there. Maybe you'll think it's strange . . . which it is . . . but I've never been there. Now, you can go there. Mills, or any other sheriff, hasn't got a thing on you. You're a gambler, an' a gambler is still more or less a respectable character in these parts. You come pretty close to bein' the most respectable citizen in this town. You can walk the streets of Rocky Point as free an' easy as you can walk from here to your cabin. Nice thing to know that, Dan."

"I've never had any trouble there," Farlin confessed.

"Of course not," said Lawson, displaying some enthusiasm. "An' you wouldn't have any trouble there. You could go over there an'"—he lowered his tone and leaned across the table—"open an account at the Stockmen's and Miners' State Bank, just as easy as not."

Farlin raised his brows. "I have my own way of taking care of my money," he said coldly, "and nobody is going to get it unless they're slick enough to snare it across the tables."

"Don't let on that you don't know what I mean," said Lawson with a frown. "You could go over there"—he lowered his voice again—"an' visit the bank two or three times, an' keep your eyes open an' report to me. I would do the rest an' cut you in for a third. You could find out more about that bank an' the lay of the land an' the best way to operate than any man I've got or could get. An' you wouldn't be handcuffed to a stud table for the next six or eight months. You'd be under cover, too. Now, shake that smart brain of yours an' figure out if it's worth it or not."

The outlaw leaned back in his chair as the waiter parted the curtains and put their breakfasts on the table.

There was no further talk until the meal was nearly finished. Lawson's eyes gleamed with satisfaction as he noted that Farlin was thinking hard.

"Have you talked much with Big Tom yet?" asked the gambler.

"Just said hello at the bar an' he told me Mills was here," was the answer.

"He'll ask you if you know a go-getter by the name of Bovert who's headed this way," said Farlin casually.

"Yeah?" Lawson scowled. "I've heard of him, that's all. Who is he anyway?"

"I don't know, and Tom doesn't know. Mills brought the word he was making for Sunrise. Funny business. Mills wants him let alone. That's the word, and all I know."

Lawson's scowl deepened. "Hasn't got anything to do with me," he said. "But I don't want any complications. I'd rather have you keep me posted than have to depend on Tom. What do you . . . think about things?"

"I don't know," said Farlin, finishing his coffee. He rolled and lit a cigarette. "How do I know you'll play square?" he asked, looking the outlaw straight in the eyes.

Lawson rose. He took a roll of bills from a pocket and tossed it on the table beside Farlin's plate. "There's twenty thousand cold," he said. "Take it over an' deposit it, for a starter."

He slipped through the curtains, leaving Dan Farlin staring at the money on the table.

Chapter Four

Dropping his napkin over the roll of banknotes, Dan Farlin called the waiter and ordered more coffee. As the waiter parted the curtains to leave, after bringing the coffee, the gambler glimpsed a familiar figure at the counter that ran the length of the room opposite the booths. It was Porky, with his spindle legs twined about a stool directly in front of the booth. Farlin's gaze hardened.

For some little time he toyed with the spoon in his coffee. He realized now that Lawson's bluster and his display of money—his disregard for money—had been a taunt. Moreover, his proposition interested Farlin mightily. Easy money and under cover. The outlaw had rung the bell when he had said that Farlin would have to slave at the tables six or eight months for the stake he needed. And Farlin had tricked him. But he, in turn, had been goaded into doing so by the outlaw leader's taunts and loud talk. The gambler stirred uneasily. It was a feeble excuse. But Lawson had again been right in saying that Farlin *had* to make his stake one way or the other. So why not . . . ?

Farlin jerked the napkin off the roll of banknotes, slipped off the rubber band, and counted them. The amount was correct. In the roll was $20,000. He snapped the rubber band back into place and put the roll of money in an inside pocket. He drank his coffee, left a $5 bill for the waiter, and stepped out of the booth.

"Ah, Porky," he said smoothly, pausing at the side of the diminutive gunman at the counter, "up all night?"

"An' that ain't unusual for me," grumbled Porky, failing to look up.

"Sheriff still in town?" Farlin inquired pleasantly, rolling a cigarette.

"Gettin' his breakfast over at the hotel," was the answer.

Farlin lit his cigarette and sat down on the stool next to the smaller man with his back to the counter. In this position he could see Porky's face. The latter was plainly nervous. He never had felt at ease in Farlin's company, but this morning he appeared less composed than usual.

"You don't usually eat in here, do you, Porky?" Farlin asked affably.

The little man's swift glance was furtive. "I eat where it's handiest," he answered. "There ain't much difference in the places in this town."

"That's right," agreed Farlin. "I usually eat at home with Gladys. What became of that fresh 'puncher I hit last night?"

"Some of the boys put him right, an' he ended up dead drunk in the hay," Porky replied readily.

"Sorry it happened," said Farlin. "Seen Lawson this morning?"

"Why, you . . ." Porky looked up startled, and a dull red came into his sallow cheeks.

"Sure." Farlin smiled. "I had breakfast with him. I was wondering if you noticed which way he went. He finished before I did." He did not believe that Porky could have overheard any of the conversation in the booth, and he had learned what he wanted to know. His smile became warm.

"Say, Porky." He leaned toward the other and glanced about swiftly. The smaller man's look of apprehension faded before the gambler's show of confidence. "Does Big Tom figure that I'm just a plain fool, or does he think I'm too slick?" Farlin put the question in an undertone.

The little gunman was startled. "What . . . how should *I* know?" he stammered, caught entirely off his guard.

"Well, why should he tell you to watch me?" Farlin asked, wrinkling his brow.

Porky's jaw fell. He saw the light in Farlin's eyes change to a cold steel-blue and knew he could not lie to this man. But no words were forthcoming. The expression in his face answered the question in Farlin's mind.

"You never have any too much money, Porky," said Farlin. "Let me pay for your breakfast. I had a good night." He tucked a bill under the edge of Porky's plate. It was so folded that the smaller man could see the figures. $100. "You don't have to say a word, Porky," said Farlin, "and I'll tell you straight that I won't. You know me. I'm not a bad sort to have on the right side, Porky. You didn't just come into this place this morning by accident, did you?"

The little gunman's palm closed over the banknote. "No," he said. "I came into this place . . . to eat." His eyes met Farlin's and the gambler nodded. "Just between you and me," said the latter. "So long." He threw away the end of his cigarette.

"So long," said Porky, looking after him as he left, with a puzzled expression on his face. This expression changed to a shrewd look when Farlin had gone out. In Sunrise parlance, Porky was a rat.

* * * * *

Big Tom Lester was in his office counting the night's receipts when Dan Farlin tapped on the door and entered unceremoniously.

"Oh, hello, Dan," Big Tom greeted with his nearest approach to a smile. He was fingering a thick stack of banknotes. "Do any good last night?"

Farlin put a roll of bills on the desk. "There's the rake-off. I changed in the heavy stuff." He indicated the piles of gold and silver on the desk and sat down in a chair to roll a cigarette.

Lester frowned. "Just a minute till I finish counting this," he said, as he resumed his task.

"No hurry," drawled Farlin. A wave of disgust had swept over him as he noted the resort proprietor's grasping fingers and the cold gleam of avarice in his eyes. It was suddenly brought home to him that he had virtually been under this man's thumb for five straight years. Handcuffed to the tables. Lawson was not a fool. There had been occasions in the distant past when Farlin had staked his all on the turn of a card. Why not a last, swift, sure play?

"Game broke up early, didn't it?"

Big Tom's rasping voice broke in on the gambler's thoughts like a thunderclap and brought a flash of resentment into the man's eyes.

"Lawson set the time limit for daylight," he said with a long, simulated yawn.

"Well, Lawson wasn't the only player in the game," said Big Tom sarcastically. "This take ain't no world-beater, either."

"The other players were men from Lawson's outfit," Dan Farlin explained easily, "and they obeyed orders. I raked off the usual percentage and drew down on the pots I won myself. I don't go out and solicit trade when a game breaks up."

"The longer a game lasts, the more you make," Lester snapped.

"Games are apt to slow up after six or seven hours," said Farlin. "I don't aim to take on any fresh crowds after seven in the morning after this."

"No?" Big Tom looked astonished. "Farlin, you're slowin' up, maybe. I've seen you play forty-eight, yes, I've seen you play as long as . . ."

"Not this spring, you haven't," Farlin interrupted. "I'm getting along, Tom. Maybe you'd better look for another mainstay to pep up these big games." This time his yawn was genuine.

Lester now was staring at him in real concern. "What's the matter?" he demanded. "Don't you feel well?"

"If you've got to know, I'm sleepy," was the cool retort.

"Bah!" snorted Big Tom. "How'd you make out last night?"

"I did well enough," Farlin answered. "Caught Ed on a few big ones. The others played rather close and Cole quit early."

"I see." Lester nodded. "What do you figure my split?"

"Your split," said Farlin slowly, "is in the take. I didn't even take the trouble to count it."

"In the take!" Lester exploded. "Since when?" He glared at Farlin angrily, and the gambler met his look coldly.

"Since midnight," he said. "When you cool down a bit, I wish you'd explain to me in a business-like way just why I should split my winnings at your tables with you. You're running a public place, are you not? I draw a certain amount of profitable trade, do I not? I protect you for your rake-off in the biggest games . . . isn't that so? Have I ever asked you to make good any of my losses? You better lock the jack up in the safe, go get some sleep, and take a tumble to yourself. And there's another little matter to take up."

Farlin paused, while Lester gripped the arms of his chair and struggled to keep back the hot words that would mean a definite break with the suave gambler.

"I saw Porky sneaking around this morning in my vicinity," Farlin continued, his eyes slightly narrowed. "Maybe I'll stand watching, but I don't like it, understand? And that isn't all, Tom." He lowered his voice impressively. "I won't stand for it."

"You're imagining things, Dan," blustered Lester. "The take is all right and I won't kick. It's only that . . . we've sort of worked together." He began putting the gold and silver into the cash box of the safe. "If you want to work entirely on your own, that's up to you, I suppose. I've always felt I supplied the . . . the material to work on, you might say. I think you gettin' mixed up in that ranch business is a mistake, but you're the doctor. Anyway, it looks like a good season that's breakin' an' it's no time for us to be fallin' out. I reckon a good sleep will do us both good."

"Glad you look at it this way, Tom," said Farlin cheerfully, rising and stepping to the door. "When Porky tells you

I had breakfast with Ed Lawson this morning, just tell him he needn't be so particular about my movements in the future. So long, Tom."

Dan Farlin didn't have to glance over his shoulder as he went out to know that Big Tom's eyes were brimming with futile rage and malice. Nor did he have to guess that in the space of time he had been in Lester's office he had been marked to go. It gave him a feeling of exhilaration and the reckless years came racing back. He still could deal the Derringer from his cuff.

He walked up to his cabin, whistling in the bright, morning sun.

The cabin was built of logs, well chinked and whitewashed. It was located in a small meadow on a slope of a ridge above the creek, with grass and trees about it, a flower bed in front, and flower boxes beneath the two front windows. Vines climbed about the little porch. It was the prettiest place of abode in town.

Farlin's Negro housekeeper opened the door for him.

"Gladys about?" he asked her as he entered the comfortable living room. He looked about appreciatively. In his heart he was fonder of this place than the big ranch house he had bought in the south.

"She's gone ridin', Mister Dan," said the housekeeper.

Farlin frowned. "So early? Does she usually go riding this early in the morning, Susan?"

"She been goin' earlier since the weather got nice, Mister Dan. I'll have your breakfast ready in a jiffy. The coffee's all made."

"I'll just take the coffee, Susan," said the gambler with a trace of irritation in his voice. "I had something to eat in town. Did Miss Louise go riding with Gladys?" He referred to Louise Smith, daughter of the proprietor of the town's general store and Gladys's best friend in Sunrise.

"Not as I saw," replied the housekeeper. "That is, she didn't come up here, Mister Dan . . . Miss Louise, I mean. Sometimes they meet downtown. They is usually together."

"Bring the coffee," said Farlin, waving her aside.

He knew Gladys was in the habit of taking a ride in the morning, and in the evening, too, when the weather was good. After all, the girl was range-born and she loved the open expanse of rolling prairie. She was an expert rider and he had procured as good a horse for her as ever put hoof in that section. But this morning he had wanted to find her at home. He had intended to tell her that he hoped they would not have to remain in Sunrise till fall. He wanted to be sure that she really wished to leave. He sipped the coffee Susan brought thoughtfully. Outwardly there had been no break with Tom Lester. But there had been a break. He smiled grimly. It was the first step.

Farlin finished his coffee and went into his room. He closed the door carefully. The snub-nosed, two-barreled Derringer slipped like magic into his right hand. He put it on the table, took off his coat, brought out his cleaning kit, and thoroughly cleaned and oiled the deadly little weapon. He slipped it under one of the pillows on his bed.

There came a light tapping at the door.

Farlin whirled. "Yes?" he called.

"Miss Louise is here, Mister Dan," said the housekeeper through the door.

"I'll be right out," said Farlin. He hastily smoothed his hair, and went out into the living room and to the front door.

Louise Smith, a blonde of about Gladys Farlin's age, was standing by her horse at the foot of the steps. "Oh, I . . . I didn't want to disturb you, Mister Farlin," she said, plainly flustered at his appearance. "I just came to see Gladys. We were going riding together."

"Why, she has already gone," said Farlin, puzzled. "Were you to meet her here?"

"I suppose so," was the hesitating answer. "She said she would wait for me. We ride out every day, and . . . maybe she's looking for me in town."

"Wait a minute," said Farlin. "Susan!" he called sharply. "What time . . . how long has Gladys been gone?" he asked when the housekeeper appeared.

"'Bout a hour, Mister Dan," replied the woman, her eyes wide. "I thought she'd gone to meet up with Miss Louise here."

"She didn't leave any word?" asked Farlin.

"No, sir, nary a word. She just took her coffee an' left before the man brought her hoss. Said she'd prob'ly meet him comin' up. Isn't it all right, Mister Dan?"

"That's all, Susan. You can go." Farlin turned to Louise Smith. "Where do you usually ride of a morning?" he asked pleasantly.

"Why, we usually ride east in the sunshine, and back along the creek," replied the girl. "I guess Gladys decided to go earlier this morning. It's the nicest morning we've had this spring, just about. I'll catch up with her outside of town." She turned to her horse.

Farlin took a step forward and stopped. When the girl had mounted, he spoke again. "It's natural I should be interested in what Gladys does," he said, smiling. "I'm her father. Do you . . . ever meet anybody on these rides?"

"Sometimes," was the answer. The girl's look of surprise was genuine. "Sometimes we meet riders going in or out of town, but we avoid them."

Farlin nodded. "I expect you'll catch up with her," he said. "And I'd like to have you girls ride together when you go out."

When she rode away, Farlin hurried into the cabin. He put on his coat and took the Derringer from under the pillow. Moving aside a picture, he put several rolls of bills in a wall safe. Then he took up his hat, left the cabin, and walked down into the town.

Chapter Five

After leaving the Red Arrow, Gladys Farlin slept but little. She learned, of course, that Lawson and his band were in Sunrise. The girls who depended upon percentage were jubilant at thought of big money to be spent, but Gladys merely viewed the prospect with disgust. She knew, too, that her father would be engaged at the table. This was disgusting, also, but it was the only life she knew on the north ranges.

She was up for coffee at dawn and the dew was still upon the grass when, attired in a smart riding habit and cap, she walked down to the livery.

"Going out to get acquainted with the sunrise," she said gaily to Jules, the French-Canadian who looked after her horse. "How's the Ghost this morning?"

"He's always ready to run," Jules answered. "There's never been a better horse in the barn, Miss Gladys. I'll have him ready in a minute."

Gray Ghost was a splendid thoroughbred, built on lines of speed rather than endurance, nervous and temperamental, but reliable. Dan Farlin had bought the gelding from a racing breeder and had paid a price. Though the animal never had been put to the test, it was generally believed that the Ghost could very easily outdistance any horse thereabouts.

Gladys rode out from town across the creek to the east plain as the sun was coming up. She had promised Louise Smith to ride with her this morning, but, after the events of the night before, she wanted to be alone. And the change in the girl as she swept out upon the prairie at a stiff gallop, with the keen morning breeze fanning a flush into her cheeks and the sun striking gold from the wisps of hair blowing from under her cap, was magical. Her eyes sparkled and she rode like youth rampant, which indeed she was. Crazy Butte was a swimming blot of pink and purple straight ahead, and Gladys traversed the open plain, spurning the trail that led south of the butte to join the road to Rocky Point, some forty miles away.

When the girl had ridden halfway to the butte, about five miles, she turned southward toward the fringe of green that marked the course of the stream from Sunrise to the river. She had thought of nothing in particular, had virtually left her lot behind in town. Now the sense of her position returned and she was conscious of a growing feeling of resentment toward her father. Handsome Dan, the gambler, he was up here, Mr. Farlin in the south. To the Crazy Butte denizens and visitors she was Handsome Dan's girl. "Wait till you hear her sing!" How often she had overheard that remark by a regular addressed to a new-comer. And how she hated it.

The cottonwoods and willows were close when she turned back along the creek. And then the unexpected happened.

Gladys was not without her dreams of romance, which the wide, free country inspired. Instinctively she reined in her mount as a horseman burst from the trees before her. First glimpse of his laughing eyes, his tall, slender figure, his graceful posture in the saddle as he brought his horse to a halt before her, the sweep of his big hat uncovering a shock of chestnut hair, told her that here was no ordinary cowpuncher or longrider or . . . no, she couldn't place him.

"And they told me this country up here was tough." The words came in a deep, musical voice and his black brows arched.

Gladys could not resist his flashing smile. "It may be tougher than you think," she heard herself saying flippantly.

He shook his head soberly. "It can't be very tough with girls like you around," he said. Then hastily: "Don't peg me as being fresh. I'm just stunned with surprise and delight, that's all." A slight bow and the smile again, and Gladys noted he was young, superbly mounted, dressed in expensive taste. The butt of the gun that protruded from the flap of the black holster on his right was ivory-mounted. On the rear of his saddle was affixed a neat pack done up in a yellow slicker. A saddlebag snuggled under his left leg. Saddle and bridle were silver-mounted. A red stone gleamed on the little finger of his left hand.

It took but a short space of time for Gladys to note these details, but each of them aroused her interest.

"Who told you this country was tough?" she asked curiously.

"Why . . . isn't that Crazy Butte over there?" the youth countered, looking to the east.

She nodded. "You're a stranger here?" she said.

"And isn't there a town called Sunrise around here close?" he asked, ignoring her suggestion.

"About five miles west on this creek," she replied.

He put on his hat. "That's where my ticket reads," he announced. "Funny pair of names, Crazy Butte and Sunrise. But there's nothing funny about you. I suppose you live around here." He nodded gravely.

Gladys laughed. "I live in Sunrise," she told him, "and there's nothing funny about that town, stranger. Whoever told you that town is tough didn't side-step the truth any. You aim to stay or just visit?"

"That'll depend," he said soberly. "You see, I don't know anybody around here except you," he added with an infectious grin.

"And you better wait until you get acquainted with me," she retorted with a toss of her head.

He rested both hands on the horn of his saddle. "Young lady," he said impressively, "my name is Jim. Not James, understand . . . just Jim." He said this with such dignity, genuine or assumed, that the girl, though tempted to giggle, didn't.

"Now," he went on, lifting his brows a trifle, "you . . . oh, by the way, have you got any relatives named Jim?"

"Not that I know of," replied Gladys, thoroughly delighted at being entertained by a strange man who was so obviously clever.

"All right," he said in a tone of finality. "From now on, as long as I'm around here, I'm the only Jim so far as you're concerned. Is that a go?"

"A . . . what?" Gladys gasped out.

"Now you'll think I'm fresh again," he complained. "You said I'd better wait till I got acquainted with you, and *how* will I get acquainted with you unless I draw you out of yourself? Here I am"—he waved a hand to the four winds—"a stranger in a strange land. I cross a creek and ride out of the trees to come upon a beautiful girl. Now just how dumb would I be if I didn't try to become acquainted with her? And you don't look so tough," he finished with another grin.

"I'm not so soft, either," she said slowly. "You act as if you'd had plenty of experience being a stranger in a strange land, and, if you get fresh in Sunrise, boy, they'll soon salt you down."

His eyes flashed with a light she had not seen in them before. "If there's anything I hate, miss, it's monotony," he said, smiling. "Will you hate me if I ask you to swap names?"

"I'm not making that kind of a trade on a chance meeting," replied Gladys. "But I would like to ask you something, and this time it's you who may think that I'm being fresh."

"Not on your life, girlie," he sang quickly. "I'll tell you anything I can . . . and ask no questions as to who you are in the bargain."

She knew it was a challenge but refused to meet it. He would learn only too soon who she was, and the thought irritated her.

"You don't have to answer me," she said. "What are you going to Sunrise for?" She turned her gaze from his direct look.

"That is a leading question," he said, "and the peculiar thing is that I don't just know. I'm up here to look around, and I've heard this place Sunrise shouldn't be missed. Does that cover it?"

"It's pretty vague," said Gladys thoughtfully. "I thought maybe you were looking for work, or something like that, although it doesn't seem so probable the more I consider it. If you're looking for what's called a good time, you can get a certain brand of it in Sunrise. I don't know why I should talk to you like this, or why I should talk to you at all. I expect you can take care of yourself. But there is a tough crowd in Sunrise, and . . . well, you can guess the rest."

She flushed as he beamed upon her. "You're the straight goods," he said impulsively. "What you're doing, girlie, is warning me to watch my step. Coming from anybody else, I might not pay much attention. But, coming from you . . . ."

"You mustn't make light of everything up here," she interrupted. "You needn't thank me, and I don't want empty compliments. I get them by the gross. You'll find out why soon enough."

"You're mistaken in the party you're talking to, miss," he said, and there was no doubting his seriousness. "I don't sprinkle empty compliments around promiscuous . . . nor idle talk, either. You're the closest to fair weather I've seen in many moons of riding. If that fact bothers you, just forget it." He looked west and straightened in the saddle.

Gladys followed his gaze and caught up her reins with a low exclamation. Two men were riding toward them at a charging gallop. From the north another rider was cutting down, and Gladys recognized her friend, Louise.

"I reckon I better be chasing along," said the stranger who called himself Jim. "Maybe this is the reception committee." There was a whimsical note in his voice. "I don't suppose anybody's barred in Sunrise," he said, looking at her with the laughing eyes she had first seen. "Remember, I met you and was asking you the way to the nearest town. It happens to be Sunrise, that's all."

"It's my father and Sheriff Mills!" Gladys exclaimed as she recognized the men. Then her head went up and her eyes flashed. "It's none of their business if . . ."

"If you want to direct a stranger, girlie," he put in. "Remember that. Take it easy and maybe I'll get a chance to see you in town. I reckon we're better acquainted now." He touched the brim of his hat in salute and quickly spurred his horse toward the oncoming riders.

Sheriff Mills held up a hand as he approached and the stranger checked his horse. He knew a sheriff when he saw one, apparently, for his interest seemed to center at once on Dan Farlin.

"Where to, stranger?" asked Mills, surveying him keenly.

"The next town," said the newcomer cheerfully. "I hear it's called Sunrise and is somewhere along the creek."

"Where are you from?" It was Farlin who put the question in a curt voice, and he knew better than to put such a query to a stranger at first meeting.

The lone rider surveyed him coolly. "I can understand the sheriff, here, asking me something," he said in a pleasant voice that belied his look, "but in your case I'll have to know who's asking for information."

Farlin's face hardened. "I happen to be the father of that young lady you were talking to down there," he said sternly.

"In that case," said the stranger with a winning smile, "I'll have to tell you that you have a very courteous daughter. She was kind enough to give me my directions. I'm from down below"—he gestured toward the south—"which covers a lot of territory. You can take your pick. I'm riding my own horse, wearing my own clothes, and I'm paying my way with my own money . . . which has passed me clean to date."

Farlin could think of no immediate reply. He saw Gladys and her friend riding toward town above them on a swell of the prairie.

"Feel the same about your name, I suppose," drawled Mills.

"My name is Jim Bond," was the reply. "And my word is as good as my name. You make your headquarters in Sunrise, Sheriff?"

"I'm close enough," said Mills dryly. He had been studying Bond intently. Now he turned to Farlin. "Reckon I'll be riding on, Dan. Your girl is safe enough. Maybe you'll want to steer this visitor into town and help him with his spending. So long."

Farlin gave the sheriff a dark look as the official rode off, and this was appreciated by Jim Bond.

"Nice party," the latter observed.

Dan Farlin favored him with a frown. The gambler was annoyed at the peculiar situation in which he found himself. After all, his daughter was the only person who could throw him off his mental balance, even temporarily, as in the present case. It now was up to him to make the best of it. He would speak to Gladys later.

"This your first trip up here?" he asked in a softer tone.

"Guilty." Jim Bond smiled. "I've heard it was fertile pasture."

Dan Farlin started. He looked at the younger man sharply. Bond was not a greenhorn. He gave indubitable evidence of wisdom and experience beyond his years. He possessed no cowhand appearance, no common personality.

"That depends on what you mean by fertile." He scowled.

"I have a hunch you could tell me anything I wanted to know," said Bond, returning Farlin's steady gaze.

The gambler was trying to shake off a wild conjecture. Could this be the famous Bovert? If so, had the sheriff recognized him?

"Maybe I could," Farlin agreed. "What do you want to know?"

"Where to put up my horse and myself in town," replied Jim Bond blandly.

"I'll show you," said the nettled Farlin. "You can ride in with me."

"And unless I'm a poor guesser, that'll be a good enough card of introduction," said Bond as they started for Sunrise.

* * * * *

41

Dan Farlin found Gladys at home when he finally reached there, angry, puzzled, already feeling sore from his swift ride.

"How'd you come to meet up with that fresh newcomer?" he demanded. "It seems to me you . . ."

"Father! Don't be silly. And what were you riding around looking for me for . . . with the sheriff? That was a spectacle. The man rode out from across the creek and asked me where the nearest town was. I suppose I should have given him a cold stare and ridden on."

"I don't suppose you ever saw him before," said Farlin, and raged at himself instantly for this senseless remark.

"No. But he talked more entertainingly than the common run that comes here," said the girl. "Maybe you'll tell me why you are acting this way all of a sudden."

Farlin changed his tactics. "You won't be bothered by the common run long," he said, evading her implied question. "Gladys, you were right. It's time we left here, and left here for good. You'll understand why I don't want you to mention this to anyone. We're going, and we're going before long. Meanwhile, I don't want you to sing any more at the Red Arrow."

The girl stared at him. "We're going?" She looked as if she could hardly believe it. There was mistrust in her eyes. "I do hope you mean it, Daddy. But I'm going to sing tonight . . . and every night until we're ready to go. Maybe that'll speed your plans. Anyway, it's final."

She went into her room, and Dan Farlin knew she meant it.

Chapter Six

When he rode into the barn, Jim Bond surveyed the livery-man from his seat in the saddle. He jerked a thumb over his shoulder toward the street.

"Can you see that gent parading out there?" he asked. "The one with the town clothes and the two big flashlights, I mean. He left his horse at the hotel."

The liveryman looked and shook his head. "Nobody out there now," he said, subjecting the newcomer to a closer examination, and looking his horse over with undisguised admiration.

"Well, no matter," said Bond lightly. "I met a man out here a piece who directed me to town and this place. I didn't ask him his name, but I'm curious. Good-looking gent, blue suit, town shoes, soft, gray hat, and sporting a big sparkler in his tie and another on his finger. A gambler I should say, maybe?"

"That would be Dan Farlin," the liveryman decided. "He'd have told you who he was, I reckon, if you'd asked him. Dan ain't got no notion or reason to keep his name quiet."

"Exactly," said Bond, dismounting and turning his reins over to the liveryman. "That would be him, I expect. I don't aim to be too curious, but I met a girl riding out west of here, and he said she was his daughter. Right-looking girl, too. Has Dan Farlin got a daughter?" A piece of gold found its way into the liveryman's palm.

"Well, I don't blame a young feller like yourself for bein' curious," said the liveryman. "Yes, Dan has a daughter by name of Gladys. She just put up her hoss. Could you tell her hoss if you saw it?"

Bond strolled down the barn a short distance and pointed out a horse. "Yes or no?" he said with his smile.

"Yes." The other grinned. "It was Gladys Farlin, all right, an' her old man is Dan Farlin. He's a gambler, like you say, but he's a square-shooter. You ain't the first visitor that has gone locoed at first sight of Gladys, but she's bad medicine for freshies, boy. Take my tip an' keep your boots shined."

"I always welcome information." Bond nodded gravely. "Take good care of my horse and you'll reap a just reward. I'll just take this pack along to the hotel and engage lodgings, breakfast, and bed, and, if anybody asks for me, don't tell 'em I'm a stranger. Just say Jim Bond is in town. I haven't any reason to keep my name quiet, either."

Bond went to the hotel, spent some time at the wash bench, shaved with hot water from the kitchen, ate a hearty meal, and went to his room for a long nap. He had not slept the night before.

* * * * *

If Dan Farlin hadn't been in such a hurry to ride out on the west plain in search of Gladys in the first place, and hadn't been so eager to call his daughter to account immediately after his return to town, he might have been interested to learn that Big Tom Lester and Ed Lawson held a conversation at the end of the bar in the Red Arrow that lasted some little time and did not serve to improve the humor of the resort proprietor.

"Now, Tom, just what're you-all tryin' to get out of me?" asked Lawson good-naturedly, after they had consumed a pair of "morning's mornings" with Lester eying the outlaw suspiciously.

"I don't just know," Big Tom confessed. "But . . . look here, Lawson, does anything seem different to you this spring?"

"Yes," replied Lawson. "You seem different, Tom. What's eatin' you, anyway?"

"Well . . ." Lester hesitated, scowled, then spoke what was in his mind. "First, Mills comes along an' tells me this Bovert is headed this way. Why should he go to that trouble? Then you come along an' order your outfit to bed at daybreak an' tell me you, of all men who come here, haven't heard of this Bovert. Then Dan Farlin acts peculiar . . . most peculiar." He nodded significantly.

"I can explain all those things," said Lawson easily. He had shown sudden interest when Lester had spoken about Farlin. "Mills don't want you to bother this Bovert because he wants a crack at him himself, for some reason. Don't ask me the reason, for I don't know an' don't care. I ordered my men to make themselves scarce because I don't want 'em puttin' on any circus while this same Mills is in town to look 'em over. He can remember faces too easy. I don't know every wild man in this country or any other, which lets me out so far as this Bovert is concerned. As for Dan Farlin, well, what's the matter with him? How does he act? He played good cards last night, so far's I could see . . . an' I saw plenty."

"Made a good winning, didn't he?" coaxed Lester.

"Why, you ought to know," said Lawson in surprise. "You get a cut, don't you? An' I don't think Dan would hold out on you any more than I think it would be good business on your part to try to check up on him an' have him find it out."

"I'm not tryin' to do that," said Lester hastily. "But Dan didn't cut me in, except for the rake-off. Now, don't tell anybody I let you in on this. Somehow I got the impression this mornin' that Dan don't care if he stays here or not, an' I don't know any place where he could do better."

Lawson's eyes were gleaming with interest. "Gettin' independent, is he? An' that makes you sore? Well, I expected it before this, Tom. I don't see that you've got any kick coming.

45

He scoops a heavy rake-off for you an' draws trade. If it wasn't for Dan Farlin amusing me at cards, I wouldn't come to this measly town. My custom's worth keepin', ain't it? An' maybe there's others feel the same way. Naturally Dan's come around to thinking what he wins should be his own. I wouldn't bother Dan if I was you, Tom."

"Oh, I won't bother him," said Lester with a heavy frown.

"You're figuring to get him sooner or later this very minute," Lawson accused with a harsh laugh. "Here, boy, fill 'em up."

Lester didn't speak again until after the drinks had been served and consumed. "It's that girl of his," he said, putting down his glass. "She's gettin' stuck up."

"I wouldn't bring her into it, a-tall," warned Lawson.

Lester looked at him quickly. "I didn't know you an' Dan was so friendly," he said with a shrewd glance.

"Is that why you had Porky trailin' us this morning?" asked Lawson coldly.

"That fool is through!" exclaimed Lester. "I don't know what you mean by his trailing you," he lied, "but he ain't on my list any more."

"How you goin' to get rid of him?" asked Lawson quietly.

"I'm goin' to tell him to get out," snarled Lester. "That'll be enough. I've still got something to say about the hangers-on in this town."

"Yeah? You talk as if you was afraid you're slipping."

"Well, I'm not," Lester snapped angrily. Then he recovered himself and realized that he had told the outlaw too much. "I'm not right this mornin', Ed. Just forget what I said, will you?"

"Sure," Lawson promised genially. "You ain't got no easy job, Tom, even if you have got a mint here. But you've got to hold your head. I'm goin' to bed. Been ridin' hard lately. So long."

His talk with Lawson left Big Tom Lester in an ugly mood. There was something between the outlaw and Farlin, Lester felt sure. Hadn't Lawson practically threatened to stay clear of the town if Farlin left? Farlin had had him guessing; now both of them had him guessing. If Porky was any good . . .

Big Tom swore, called for another drink from his private stock, tossed it off, and left the place. Farlin had long since ridden off by chance with Sheriff Mills and had just returned. The resortkeeper would have welcomed sight of Porky to question him, but he had no thought of looking him up. He would have to be back at his place of business by 2:00 that afternoon. He went home.

* * * * *

The sun was slanting low in the west when Jim Bond woke. He was up and out speedily for a look at his horse and a bite to eat. He strolled about town, dropping in at the various resorts, until after sunset, and, with the coming of night, went back to the Red Arrow, which he had recognized at once as the liveliest place in town.

Lawson's outfit, having been told to go a bit easy against a prospective early departure, was abroad. Red Cole was in command. Farlin was standing with Big Tom at the latter's customary station at the lower end of the bar near the door to the little office. Big Tom was scowling and appeared nervous. He had had a talk with Porky finally, and it had not been satisfactory. But he had not ordered the little gunman out of town. Again and again his thoughts reverted to Lawson's intimation that he had talked as if he felt himself slipping. He believed he hated both Lawson and Farlin. They were too smart. Porky was dumb, but he might have more use for him. In any event, this was no way for the money season to start.

"This looks like a live one," Farlin remarked suddenly.

Big Tom glanced quickly in the direction the gambler indicated and saw Jim Bond, tall, handsome, swaggering, playing large gold pieces at the nearest wheel. Bond had seen Farlin at once and had stopped at the roulette table where he could watch him for a spell.

"Number three, red," the croupier droned, and shoved two stacks of gold beside the winning piece.

Bond laughed, took one of the stacks, and left the other on the number for a repeat. The croupier's eyes glanced toward Big Tom, and the latter frowned.

"Twenty-dollar limit at this table," said the croupier, paying the bets on the color and taking the losing wagers.

"That's not so much," taunted Jim Bond. "Where's the sky-limit layout?"

"I'm only running this table," was the reply. "Make your bets, gents. Here goes the little ball."

Jim Bond took up the gold pieces and put them in a side pocket of his coat. He turned and walked to the bar, edging in close to Farlin. He held up a finger authoritatively at a white-coated servitor. Then he noticed Farlin and his eyes lighted.

"Have one with me?" he invited.

"Go ahead," said Big Tom in an undertone. "Looks like ready money in a strange place."

Dan Farlin moved beside Bond. "I'll take one and ask a question," he said in a pleasant voice.

"And I'll answer it and ask one back," said Bond with a keen look at Lester. "But first, should I ask the pouty-looking boss in?"

Farlin smiled. "I wouldn't take in too much territory on short notice," he advised. "Few people ask Big Tom to drink, and he drinks with fewer than that."

"Must be tough to have a grouch and a mint at the same time," Bond observed.

Farlin had noticed his clear eyes, his clean features, and had decided he was not a braggart or a fool.

"You seem to think you know quite a bit about people at first sight," he said dryly, raising his glass.

"I don't exactly jump at conclusions," said Bond slowly. "Would you want to know what I thought of you when I first saw you?"

"No," replied Farlin shortly. "Here's to green grass. You hinted you were looking for fertile pasture."

Jim Bond gave him a swift look. "Now for the question?" he said, dropping a silver dollar on the bar and spinning another after it with a graceful gesture.

"What was your idea in making that big play at the wheel for my benefit?" asked Farlin quietly, keeping his eyes on the other.

Bond's teeth flashed in a smile. "Love me, love my dog," he bantered. "That play wasn't made for your benefit, Mister Farlin. I didn't even know you were looking. I was drilling to bedrock to see how high the limit might be. That's the right answer. Should I put my question now?"

"Go ahead." Farlin nodded with a cold smile. "But this doesn't mean I'm believing your answer."

"Your privilege," said the young buckaroo, tapping the bar with the strong, slender fingers of his right hand—a gun hand if Farlin ever had seen one. "Can you tell me if a fellow can get a little strong play hereabouts that's not too raw? The man who told me your name said you were on the level."

"That was kind of him," said Farlin. "I don't suppose you inquired of anyone besides the liveryman." The question was in the tone in which he spoke.

"Didn't think it necessary," said Bond a bit sharply. "You see, I had already formed a first impression."

Dan Farlin was interested. This youth was no boy; he was far from inexperienced. The gambler suspected that he had appraised Big Tom more accurately than he had let on. He could hold his own in a conversation that had double and triple meanings. He could talk between the lines, which meant fast thinking and quick convictions—a subtle and sometimes dangerous combination.

"How strong a game are you looking for?" he asked.

"Strong enough to put a proper value on the cards and the way they're played," was the ready answer.

"There'll be a game of stud with those earmarks later," Farlin said thoughtfully. "Maybe I can get you in," he added in sudden decision, "but it's a tough lay."

"I'll take a chance," said Bond. "It won't be any worse . . ." He stopped speaking as a hush came over the room. The pianist began to play and a girl began to sing. Bond turned quickly and stood with his right arm outstretched along the bar until Gladys Farlin had finished. He did not join in the applause, made no attempt to shower gold pieces into the velvet-lined basket on the platform. But he did catch the singer's eye.

He looked soberly at Dan Farlin. "That's what she meant when she said I'd find out who she was soon enough," he said. "I suppose she thought I . . ." He frowned and ceased.

"Yes?" prompted Farlin, eyeing him closely.

"It doesn't matter," Bond said with a shrug. "Mister Farlin, will you play the game and introduce me to your daughter, or do I have to sneak one behind your back?"

Dan Farlin looked at him steadily for some moments. No man could tell what was going on in his mind. "Come with me," he said, compressing his lips.

He led the way through the throng and into a narrow passage behind the dance floor. There they waited until Gladys came hurrying to her room, the place rocking with applause.

"Gladys," said her father, "meet Mister Jim Bond."

"How do you do?" said Gladys, glancing quickly from one to the other of the two men, a bit flustered, evidently surprised.

"The best I can, Miss Farlin," said Bond with a slight bow.

"And now we'll see about our game," said Dan Farlin with a hint of enthusiasm.

Gladys's eyes widened, then she turned abruptly and left them.

"We'll have to call that fair, I suppose," said Jim Bond grimly, "but she'll think you introduced me for . . . selfish reasons. I'll do what I can to straighten it out . . . later."

Farlin whirled on him, his eyes narrowed. "You'll . . ." He caught himself in time as the other smiled in his face.

"We'll see about our game, as you put it," said Bond in a soft, purring voice. "It wouldn't do for you and me to quarrel."

Dan Farlin still was trying to think up an answer to this as they made their way back to the floor of the big resort.

Chapter Seven

When they approached the bar, Farlin saw Red Cole leaving Big Tom Lester at the latter's station near the office door. "Hang around," the gambler said to Bond in a swift aside. Then he disengaged himself and casually joined the resort proprietor.

Lester grinned at him. "Got him rigged for a game?" he asked in as genial a tone as he could manage.

"Maybe," Farlin replied shortly. "He's plenty smart, though. What's on Red's mind?" He glanced sharply at the big man.

"He wanted to know who your friend was." Lester chuckled. "You know, nothing gets by Cole."

"Nothing except a danger signal," remarked Farlin dryly. "And if I'm not mistaken, he'll get one soon if he monkeys around over there." He nodded toward the roulette table where Bond was again preparing to play, with Cole edging in beside him.

Lester looked and frowned. "He hasn't got any orders from me," he said, half to himself. "Cole an' you have some trouble in the game last night?"

Farlin glanced at him coldly. "Lawson tell you that Cole flew off the handle because he was losing?" he inquired.

Lester shook his head. "Some of the others mentioned it, an' it got around," he said. "You know such things won't keep, Dan. By the way, I'd like for you to run the game tonight as usual. You don't have to cut your winnings if you feel that way about it. I'm not cheap, Dan. I suppose you've got a game comin' up."

"Don't know a thing about it," said Farlin. "Haven't seen Lawson since this morning, and . . . listen, Tom, I'm going to lay off for a couple of days when Lawson's outfit beats it."

"Yeah?" Lester looked startled. "What's the matter, Dan? I don't believe you're feelin' good, although you sure look all right."

"I feel as good as you say I look." Farlin frowned. "I've got some personal business to attend to, that's all. I may run out of town, and I'll expect you to look out for Gladys while I'm gone. Maybe she won't sing for a night or two, but I'm not sure."

Lester now was genuinely alarmed and showed it. "Come in the office, Dan," he invited, turning toward the door.

"No." Farlin halted him. "It isn't necessary to go in there, and it doesn't look good for us to be having so many private talks. I don't want to start this Lawson outfit wondering."

Lester turned back to the bar, biting his lip in perplexity. Finally he looked squarely at the gambler.

"Dan, let's have a showdown," he said. "You ain't figuring on blowing the town, are you? Because if you are . . . that is . . ."

"If I am, I should give you a chance to fill my place, eh?" said Farlin grimly. "That's what you mean, isn't it? You've had that chance a long time, Tom. If you'd known anybody who could run these big games better, or who would run 'em as square, you'd have tried to get rid of me long ago. I don't have to give you notice if I want to blow this town, and I'm on my own from here on in."

Lester remembered what Lawson had said about not visiting the place again if Farlin left. Other good customers might feel the same way.

"Don't get me wrong," he said in a smooth voice. "It's only that I don't want you to go, Dan. An' I can't see where you could do any better anywhere else. Make what you can, an' give me my rake-off, an' I'll be satisfied."

Both looked toward the roulette table as a clear, cold voice reached their ears. Jim Bond and Red Cole were standing back a pace from the table, looking at each other.

ROBERT J. HORTON

"You one of the bosses here?" Bond asked sharply.

"That's for you to find out," Cole retorted with a sneer.

Bond looked at the croupier. "Didn't you tell me a while ago that twenty dollars was the limit?" he demanded.

"That was before ten o'clock," replied the houseman, looking past him at Big Tom, who gave no sign.

"I see." Bond nodded. "The limit changes every hour . . . is that it?" The last words cracked in the air.

"Suppose it does?" purred Red Cole as a hush fell over the room. "That reason enough to kick on my bet?" He put his hands on his hips and thrust his chin forward.

"It might be," Bond retorted. "Did anybody ever tell you how you act right free with strangers?"

"If they get fresh, I put 'em where they belong," said Cole.

Bond laughed—at least the spectators thought it was a laugh. Lester knew better, and he started forward as Dan Farlin caught his arm and drew him back. "Let's see what this youngster's got," said the gambler for Lester's benefit alone. The big man halted. But Cole had seen this little by-play out of the corner of his eye. He had seen Farlin disappear with the stranger for a short space, too. Cole's dislike for Farlin had changed to hatred in the early morning hours. The man before him might be a friend of Farlin's.

"You won't be bothered putting me in my place," Jim Bond was saying, "I'm already there."

Someone in the crowd chuckled, and Cole's face darkened. "If you're lookin' for trouble, you've come to headquarters, you . . ."

"Don't call me any names." Everyone in the place and even in the street outside heard the words distinctly. Bond left his annoyer no alternative whatsoever.

"You . . . you . . ." Cole was inarticulate with the rage swelling within him. He caught sight of the calm, handsome face of Farlin. "You son-of-a-bitch."

55

The epithet hardly had time to escape the bully's lips when Bond's left palm smacked across his mouth. The slap sounded like a crash of glass to the stunned onlookers. It was so unexpected that Big Tom Lester shouted involuntarily: "Don't draw!"

The warning was too late, so far as Bond was concerned, and was not needed by Cole, for Bond's gun was in his hand, held steady at his hip, and none present had seen the move, except, possibly, Dan Farlin.

"Now we understand each other," said Bond. "What is it . . . peace or war? I came here for a visit, and I haven't changed my mind. If anybody snapped you onto me, that goes for him, or them, too. Do we both stay, or does one of us stay alone?"

This time Lester did not hesitate, and Farlin did not attempt to stop him. The big man stepped between the principals in the drama with three swift strides. "Cut it out!" he roared. "That goes for you, too, Red. I mean it."

A number of Lawson's other men had crowded behind Cole, and Bond had noted their hostile looks. Two or three of them whispered to Cole. And at this moment the music struck up and the voice of Gladys Farlin floated clearly in song.

The interruption had its effect in disconcerting Cole and his followers. The murmur of voices rose to a pitch that drowned the words he spoke to Bond. The latter merely threw back his head with a short laugh, sheathed his gun like magic, and turned to the table. Cole moved away and was soon hemmed in at the bar.

Lester stood irresolutely while the girl finished the short song. He eyed Bond narrowly as the newcomer resumed his play for higher stakes. Then he spoke to Farlin, who had followed him.

"He just got here," he said. "Did you see that draw? Fast as light. Maybe it's Bovert." He paused, asking Farlin the question with his eyes.

"If it is, you'd better leave him alone," said Farlin with a faint smile. "He's too fast for Cole, and that means he's too fast for you. I reckon he can take care of himself without your ordering him to be left alone." The gambler turned away and strolled out of the place.

Farlin walked rapidly down the street to a small house that was set back between two other buildings. As he reached it, Ed Lawson came out the door and closed it quickly behind him. The outlaw stopped short as Farlin hailed him in a low voice.

"Hello, Dan. Startin' the roundup for the night this early?" he greeted.

"No," returned the gambler. "Go down to the Arrow and take a look at what just blew in. Anybody'll point him out to you. He just called Red proper, and made Red take it. If you can place him, I want to know for my own reasons."

"Sure," Lawson consented. "Ain't this bloodthirsty gent you're lookin' for, is it?"

"Might be," growled Farlin. "Take a look-see, Ed. And do me a favor, will you . . . without asking any questions?"

"That'll depend," said Lawson, looking puzzled.

"Call off the high play for tonight," said Farlin.

Lawson's bushy brows went up. "You don't want to play?" he said in amazement. He peered closely at Farlin's face. "What's behind it, Dan?"

"I may go away for a day or two," Farlin finally replied.

"I see." Lawson's eyes gleamed with comprehension. "Maybe I'll take my bunch out for a week or so." He nodded. "An', by the way, Dan, Lester told me you was actin' sort of queer, an' I told him to handle you with silk gloves, so he understood . . . see?"

"Thanks," said Farlin wryly, and walked rapidly away.

Meanwhile, with Farlin absent—a coincidence that annoyed him—Big Tom found opportunity to speak privately to Porky Snyder.

"I'm giving you a last chance," he told the evil-eyed gun-toter. "You might as well know it. It won't be hard for you to figure out that it'll be wise to stay jake with me, an' this time it means a couple of hundred in your pocket, maybe five, but I ain't promising till I see how you perform."

Porky looked about the card room, deserted but for the two of them, avoided Lester's eyes, and stared at the blank wall with a queer expression, as if he saw the handwriting upon it. He flashed a single glance at his boss.

"I know what you're thinkin'," said Big Tom quickly in a whispering voice, "but you couldn't get away with it, Porky. In the first place, you wouldn't gain anything by bumping me off in the dark, an' in the second place you ain't got nerve enough to do it. You fall down in a big pinch, Porky, an' you know it. Oh, you've got notches in your gun, but how'd you get 'em? You'd be runnin' with Lawson right now if Lawson would have you. But he don't want you. You can't go out on your own because you ain't got the brains. I've looked after you for five years or so an' you'd starve to death if you left or anything happened to me now." The speaker lighted a cigar and missed the flash of fire in Porky's eyes. It was not always best to be too frank with a man like this. The taunt found its mark and Porky trembled with suppressed desire. Lester did not realize he was treading dangerous ground.

"Listen hard," said Lester with a scowl, "an' don't let what you hear go any farther than that door." He put a huge hand on the smaller man's arm and gripped him. "Farlin is goin' away for a day or two, he tells me," he said, lowering his voice. "Hinted he might go out of town . . . on business. There's only one place I've ever known him to go when the season was on, an' that's Rocky Point. I want to know if he does go there, an' I want you to hang out in the trees along the creek to see. That's worth the two hundred I mentioned. If you can find out what he goes there for, if he does go there, it'll be worth the five hundred I also mentioned. An' I don't care if he sees you or not so long as you get back to report."

Porky rubbed the side of his nose, thinking. "I've got to know if you an' Farlin are still . . . still all right," he murmured.

"You've got to know what I tell you, an' that's all," said Lester angrily. "You can take this on or not. Suit yourself." He turned to the door. "But remember . . ."

"Forget it," said Porky in a tone the big man never before had heard him use. "Gimme some expense money."

With an oath, Lester drew out a roll of bills and handed one to him. "There's fifty," he growled. "Tell yourself that's got to be enough an' you'll be playin' safe."

He stepped out of the room into the narrow corridor at the rear of the main room and stopped short with another oath. The newcomer was strolling ahead of him. He strode toward him and touched him on the arm.

"Was you lookin' for something in here?" he asked, glowering into the other's eyes.

"Yes," said Bond, brightening. "I thought maybe a tall game might be operating somewhere back here and needing a customer."

The ready, suave reply was disarming. The stranger had given every indication of wanting to gamble, and to gamble strong. Where was Farlin?

"What's your name?" Lester demanded. "I'm the big shot around here."

"Name's Bond . . . Jim Bond," was the reply, without an instant's hesitation. "And I knew you were the big gun first sight."

"Huh!" snorted Lester. Confound that man Mills! "You seem to know Farlin. Didn't he tell you maybe you could get accommodated?"

"Well, where is he?" was the eager counter-question.

"Hang around," said Lester, unconsciously repeating Farlin's admonition. He frowned heavily, for there were a number of queries he would have liked to put to the man who regarded him so coolly. "Stay out in front," he ordered, and looked behind to make sure that Porky had not yet left the card room.

"Sure," said Bond. "Maybe it would help if you slipped him the good word." He walked on ahead of Lester, while the latter motioned with his hand at his side lest Porky should follow them.

But Porky had no intention of following. He had listened at the door to the verbal exchange between Lester and Bond and had stolen a look at the stranger who he had seen draw down on Red Cole. The incident had been a source of gratification, for he disliked Cole and believed Lawson's lieutenant had prevented him from joining the outlaw's band. He turned back into the room and closed the door. He sat down at the table and drew a pack of cards from a side pocket of his coat. He shuffled them and began to deal solitaire.

Porky Snyder no longer was young. Big Tom's words had rankled and stung because they had carried the edge of truth. Porky realized only too well that he had been, and was at that minute, dependent on the proprietor of the Red Arrow. His eyes narrowed; he stopped dealing and stared thoughtfully at the blank wall. There had been some sort of a break between Lester and Farlin. Otherwise, why should Lester be so interested in Farlin's movements all of a sudden? And, while Porky had been spying for Lester, he also had been seeing a thing or two for himself and jumping at conclusions. He had seen Farlin and Lawson in conference. They had talked so low he could not hear a word in the restaurant, and that meant they were speaking confidentially. There had been every indication that the two were on exceptionally friendly terms. Porky's eyes glistened. How would he choose, if given an opportunity, between Lester and the other two? He smiled to himself. Moreover, if there had been a break between the gambler and Lester, it could mean but one thing—one or the other would have to leave town. Now, Farlin was going away for a day or two. Lester hadn't said when; that was for Porky to learn. He would have to be ready. But there was a more important thought in the little gunman's brain. He had been given a last chance. Why should he stay? If he could get hold of some money—a good sum of money . . .

The door opened and Farlin stepped inside. Behind him came Red Cole and others of Lawson's outfit, and Jim Bond. The gambler, in the lead, scowled.

"Beat it!" he ordered in a tone of contempt.

"An' make it fast," Cole put in, his hand dropping to his gun.

Porky slipped out, noting a curious look on the face of the stranger, Bond.

Cole swept the cards Porky had left on the table to the floor with a curse. When the newcomers were seated, every chair of the seven about the table was occupied.

"A thousand-dollar change-in?" asked Farlin, breaking open a new pack of cards.

Before anyone could reply, the door opened and Ed Lawson's big form loomed in the doorway. Two men rose, each offering his place. Farlin looked up, apparently but mildly interested, and saw Big Tom Lester peering over Lawson's shoulder with a scowl on his face.

"Never mind," said Lawson to the two men who were standing, "I'm not taking a hand." He looked at Cole and shook his head. "No game," he said sternly.

"What's that?" cried Cole in astonishment.

"You heard me," said Lawson sternly, his eyes narrowing. "I said, no game! We're leaving town."

Cole rose, his face dark. He wet his lips, looked from Farlin to Bond, and back at Lawson.

Lawson jerked his head toward the door. "I'll follow you boys out," he said sharply.

Cole nodded to the others and went out, with the Lawson men following and the outlaw leader himself bringing up the rear.

Jim Bond leaned back in his chair, looking from Farlin to Lester, and burst into laughter. "I reckon there's more than one boss in this joint," he said loudly. Another tantalizing outburst drove Lester from the room.

Chapter Eight

A silver moon, full and bright, rode high in the eastern sky. Yellow beams of lamplight streaked the main street of Sunrise, but elsewhere the deep shadows closed in under the trees. There was a square of orange in the window of the Farlin cabin, denoting a light left on in the living room against the return of Gladys. The air was still and sweetly scented.

There was a flutter of white on the wide path that led up the slope above the trees to the Farlin abode. Then a dark figure was outlined in the moonlight and both became motionless.

"Good evening, Miss Farlin." It was Jim Bond's voice.

"Isn't this a . . . strange appearance?" said Gladys coldly.

"Not at all," Bond assured her. "I just had to see you and have a word with you after the way we were introduced, that's all."

"Don't you suppose I know how we came to be introduced?" The girl's tone carried a hint of scorn. "That was the first time my father ever introduced me to a man like you in this town. Oh, I don't blame him. I know my father is a gambler. It seemed natural enough in the beginning, but tonight he had to introduce you in order to get you into a game. Every man has his price . . . I've found that out, Mister Bond."

"Maybe so," Bond agreed. "But my price is higher than you think. I told your dad I would clear this thing up and put him right. He didn't like the idea a little bit, but I don't see how he can help himself. He's not a bad sort, and he wasn't bribed in any such way as you think, Miss Gladys."

"I don't think he has to have you speak for him," said Gladys in a haughty voice, "and I'm not going to listen to any . . ."

"But you'll notice that I'm not sitting in any game," Bond interrupted. "I won't take the credit for that because there isn't going to be any game of the kind I want tonight. But I'll take the credit for getting the introduction to you tonight, or share it with your dad, if you want it that way. He'll talk plenty for himself, and probably plenty against me, when the time comes. Anyway, I hope so. Listen, Miss Gladys." He took a step nearer. "I asked your dad pointblank for that introduction. I asked him if he would give it to me or if I would have to sneak one behind his back. He decided to take the step himself. There was no bargain."

"I see," said Gladys. "But there's something I don't know." It was plain she was helplessly puzzled. And this stranger was in deadly earnest in his speech.

"If there is, it's on your side of the fence," said Jim Bond slowly. "I only know I liked you from the moment I set eyes on you. That's why I wanted to get acquainted right. And I'm not out here in the moonlight with a mouthful of sweet nothings to toss away."

"I think you've spoken your piece," said Gladys with a toss of her head.

He put a hand on her arm as she started to move away. "Why be mean to me, Miss Gladys? In a place like this you can't have too many friends. I might come in handy. You'll have to take me as you find me, but I'm not a bad sort. You remember you started to sing tonight just when it looked like that Cole *hombre* would be fool enough to try to draw?"

"I sing three times every night," flared the girl, but her tone betrayed her.

"But not at just such times," said Bond. "You might say it was a crisis you stepped into tonight, Miss Gladys. Yes, that was it. You stopped something. Did you do it on purpose?"

"I don't have to stand here answering ridiculous questions," replied Gladys heatedly. But Bond saw a flush mantle her cheeks.

"Wouldn't I be a fine sort not to appreciate a favor?" he said. "You don't have to answer that. Maybe I'm guessing a lot, but I don't think so. You don't usually sing when there's a gun play about to break, do you? You needn't answer that, either. But the fact remains, Gladys Farlin, that you don't want me to come to grief in Sunrise. There isn't any answer to that." He closed with a note of triumph in his voice.

"You say there's no game such as you want tonight?" she asked, changing the subject abruptly.

"No game," he answered. "That's just what the big fellow said when we were about to start. And what he said went, and went cold."

"You mean Big Tom Lester said that?"

"Nope. The other big one. The man they call Lawson."

"Oh!" There was a world of meaning in that word. "Was Father there?"

"He was to be master of ceremonies. He told me after they had gone out of the room, all but me and him, that I had been lucky to get in, and I was luckier to get out. Nice sociable place, this. But I like your dad, and I'm not saying that to try and plug up my stock."

"Lawson stopped the play?" There was undisguised wonder in Gladys's tone.

"I'll tell you," said Bond impulsively, "and this will have to be between you and me, that's all, whether you like it or not. This town seems to be moving along quiet enough on the outside. But the inside is coming to a boil, Miss Gladys. You know more about the parties concerned, and I'm only judging from what I see and hear. I can always learn a lot by just looking on. There's some kind of a polite row in progress. I've seen these rows start polite and end tragic. This one has the earmarks of being a healthy youngster."

"I don't think much of your judgment," said Gladys, but she was really thinking of her father's announcement that they were to leave the Crazy Butte range. And he had acted queerly of late. She knew, too, that trouble of the character hinted by Bond was dangerous.

"If it wasn't . . . well, ordinarily I wouldn't be interested in this business, Miss Gladys," said Bond with a frown. "I don't go around looking for trouble, and I don't go around roping introductions to every girl I meet, or making 'em myself, for that matter. But I just want you to feel that I'd be glad to be on hand if you wanted me for anything. Understand?"

"You're a gunman," said Gladys thoughtfully.

"That's according to how you look at it," he said quickly. "I'm handy with my gun, yes . . . but only when I have to be, like tonight. They told me afterward, and were careful about it, that this Cole is dynamite."

"He runs with Lawson," said the girl.

"And Lawson runs a tough outfit." Bond nodded. "That makes the cards lay right for big doings, if they get started. Are you . . . going home?"

"I live up there."

Bond looked at the orange square of light, while she studied his profile against the moonlight. Bond started. He had seen a shadow clearly outlined against the light in the window of the cabin. He looked at her quickly. "Any menfolk live up there with you?" he asked.

"My father . . . ," she began, but stopped with a sharp intake of breath. "I don't see how it concerns you," she finished severely.

"Maybe you will soon," he said, taking her arm. "Step into the shadow of these trees . . . and *wait!*"

Gladys did as she was told without thinking, impressed by his change of manner. He left her immediately, stealing up the slope in the shadows. But Gladys was not the kind to remain inactive. As soon as she recovered from her surprise, she also started up the slope. She had now lost sight of Bond, and her second surprise came when she saw a horse standing with reins dangling ahead. She looked quickly up at the cabin. No one was in sight. The housekeeper had gone to bed. It was her habit to retire early and get up to give Gladys something to eat when she got home after midnight. The girl saw at a glance that the horse was not her father's. And her father certainly had not gone home, even if there wasn't a big game in progress. She hurried on, careful to keep well in the shadows of the sparse timber below the cabin.

Jim Bond had slipped stealthily to the shadow of a large lilac bush at a corner of the cabin. The light from the front window slanted across the yard. The house was still. He also had seen the horse. Now he crept along the side of the cabin to the rear. There was an open space here between the cabin and a fringe of trees behind it. Bond waited for a while, glancing keenly about. Then he sidled along the rear wall until he reached an open window. He listened and heard faint sounds within, finally a muttered curse. Then came silence.

Bond was about to climb through the window when a form came scrambling out. Bond made a flying leap and grasped the intruder, but he did not secure a good hold. In another instant the two men were struggling on the ground, rolling over and over, each trying to grasp the other's throat. The intruder was a smaller man than Bond, quicker, harder to hold—slippery as an eel. He bit Bond's arm, and Bond reared back, losing his hold. In the instant that followed a ball of fire burst almost in Bond's face, the hot powder searing his left cheek.

Bond flung himself aside as a second tongue of red spurted. It was impossible to grasp his assailant's wrist in the short space in which the shots were fired, but Bond had secured his own gun and now brought its barrel crashing down upon the face of the man to his side.

He leaped to his feet. "Drop it or I'll give it to you!" he cried. But the other had got upon his knees, and again the gun spit its blaze of fire. Bond saw the small figure clearly in the moonlight and his own weapon cracked once, knocking the intruder backward as he was rising.

The housekeeper was screaming at the front door. A flutter of white showed at the corner of the cabin.

"Go back there!" Bond commanded sternly. "I'll bring him around into the light."

He picked the man up by the shoulders and carried him around the cabin to where the colored housekeeper, still screaming, her eyes rolling, was holding the lamp just outside the door. Shouts came from the town and men were coming up the path on the run. As Bond got his captive into the circle of light, he recognized the small man he had seen follow Lester into the card room earlier that night. It was Porky Snyder.

Bond put his burden down and speedily found the wound in the gunman's side. Suddenly there were men about him. He looked up to see Farlin, Lawson, Red Cole, and several others. At this moment, Big Tom Lester pushed his way forward.

"What's this?" he demanded, his breath coming in short gasps as he looked down at the motionless form with a curious expression in his eyes. "It's Porky!" He looked quickly at Dan Farlin.

"What was he doing here?" asked Farlin sternly.

"Just a minute!" It was Gladys's voice, and the group made way for her. "He broke into the house," the girl told her father, "and I shot him."

The men stared at the small, ivory-mounted revolver in her hand.

In a moment, Big Tom had wrenched the weapon from her grasp with an oath. But Dan Farlin pressed the muzzle of his Derringer against the big man's stomach.

"Give me the gun!" he commanded.

Lester yielded the weapon, his eyes blazing from a pale face.

"Now," said Farlin, "what was he doing here?"

"I . . . don't know," said Lester, and there was truth in his voice.

"Maybe you'd better let me say something," Jim Bond put in coolly. "I found this man climbing out of a back window and tackled him. He . . . ."

"And how did you come to be here?" Farlin demanded in a tone that was cold as ice but which trembled with frustrated anger.

"I was settling our unfinished business," shot Bond. "Don't look at that gun in your hand. Here . . ." He drew his own weapon and broke it. Then he held it out to the other. "Look at mine!" he said sharply.

"And you, mister . . . look at *this!*" said Cole.

It was Lawson who knocked the gun from Cole's hand and followed it with a crashing blow on the jaw. "This isn't our affair," he told the man on the ground a moment later. "We'll be going."

"Take him down with you," Farlin directed some of the men, pointing to the form on the ground. "Gladys, go into the house. You and I will talk this over, Tom. And you"—he nodded to Jim Bond—"can go."

Chapter Nine

Sheathing his weapon, Jim Bond surveyed Farlin coolly. Three of Lawson's men picked up the motionless form of Porky Snyder, but, as they carried him away, none of the others offered to move. Lawson gave a sharp command as Cole rose, glowering savagely, from the ground and confronted his chief. Lawson beckoned him and started away without another look. But Cole's eyes met Bond's for an instant as he turned to follow. Bond's features were set and cold. There were now three of them—Farlin, Big Tom Lester, and Bond.

"Are you going?" Dan Farlin demanded.

"Your man Porky isn't dead," said Bond. "If you don't want to take my word for it that I shot him, he'll probably tell you so himself. I want you to get this thing straight." He looked the gambler squarely in the eyes.

"I'll take your word for it," Farlin snapped. "I won't even bother to ask you how you came to be here. You're just a meddling young whelp and you're setting your own trap."

"If I am, I'll spring it," Bond retorted. "I saw this Porky snooping around up here. He's got a horse cached just below here. Maybe he told your friend Lester where he was going . . . afterward."

Big Tom swore. "I'm givin' you till daylight to get out of town!" he said harshly. "That goes, whoever you are."

Bond chuckled softly, looking steadily at Farlin. "That's supposed to scare me, I take it," he said, his expression changing with

71

the words. "Tom, you're a joke . . . and it's time somebody put you wise."

Big Tom's face went black and his right hand darted down. But Farlin caught him just in time and whirled him around. Bond's laugh echoed again. His weapon had come into his hand like a flash of light. "Suppose we cut these parlor theatricals," he suggested mildly. "If we understand each other, Farlin, I'll be going."

"That's what I'm waiting for you to do," said Farlin.

"So long." Bond nodded, with a swift glance at the enraged Lester. He put up his gun and walked jauntily down the wide trail.

"Come in the house," Farlin told Lester, and the two went inside.

* * * * *

In the shadowy space in the rear of the Red Arrow, Lawson halted and scowled at Cole.

"What was the idea in the two plays against this Bond?" he asked in a hard voice.

"Oh, is he a friend of yours?" Cole countered with a sneer. "Your pal, Tom, said to try him out, an' he tries to make a fool out of me! Maybe he did. I suppose I'm to let him get away with it. He punctures Porky, an' you let him get away with it. He . . ."

"Shut up!" commanded Lawson. "Look here, Red, I've got a reason for anything I do. Tom is just fool enough to put something off on you that he's afraid to do himself. When he puts something off on you, he's puttin' it off on me. Ever think of that? I said we'd go slow this trip, an' you try to gum up the works. I'm just askin' you one thing, Red . . . are you takin' orders or not?"

Cole's eyes were glittering beads of fire. His chief was calling him, and there was no side-stepping the issue.

"Meaning just what, Ed?" he managed to get out.

"Meanin', are you runnin' with the outfit or goin' on your own?" Lawson shot back. "If you're runnin' with me, you're takin' my orders without askin' any questions or talkin' back. If you're on your own, you're on hostile territory. You can take it or leave it. That ought to be plain enough." Lawson was not mincing words, and it was evident he was fighting mad about the whole business.

Red Cole's look of anger gave way to astonishment. "That's strong talk, Ed," he said, recovering his natural voice. "You said plenty then. Are you givin' me my notice?" His eyes narrowed.

"I'm ready to give you your orders, if you're ready to take 'em," Lawson retorted. "If you're not . . . it's the other thing. An' Big Tom's business is none of ours. We've got a big play comin' up, an' it'll be all we can do to attend to our own affairs. This is no time to be settlin' a personal grudge. I'm not anxious to lose you . . . I'll tell you that. But this newcomer might get you, whether you think so or not. Which way do you stand?"

"With you, if we're the same as always," growled Cole. "But I'd like to know . . . ."

"Get the men together an' ready to ride," ordered Lawson. "No more town stuff. We'll talk things over later. We're beating it in an hour."

Red Cole made rather a ridiculous figure, swaying and working his hands in indecision. Then, with an effort, he straightened.

"All right," he said finally, "but this is the first time you've worked behind my back, Ed, an' maybe I could be of help."

"If you could think hard enough, you'd have tried to kill me an' go out on your own long ago," sneered Lawson. "I'm your bread an' butter, an' you know it. Do as I say an' leave the big stuff to me."

"Sure," said Cole. "Sure thing." He walked away quietly enough, but there was murder in his eyes.

But if there was murder in Red Cole's eyes, there was that and more in the gaze Lawson leveled at his retreating form. The outlaw strode swiftly into the rear of the resort, but did not go into the big room. He waited possibly two minutes, and then slipped out and into the shadow of the trees behind the place. The sound of voices had come to him, and now he was waiting for Lester.

* * * * *

Whether Bond suspected anything or not, he did not keep to the trail on the way from the Farlin cabin. He entered the timber and came out upon the main street of the town at a point above the Red Arrow. Then he strolled to the livery barn. He stepped quickly into the little front office when he saw the activity within. Men were saddling horses, talking, swearing—the Lawson outfit was preparing to quit town.

As Bond had a horse that would attract any rider's eye, he proposed to see that it was not taken by mistake, or otherwise. But swift as his move had been, he had not escaped the alert glance of Red Cole, who had just arrived with Lawson's orders.

Cole watched his chance to slip into the office unobserved. The place was unlighted, except for the feeble rays of the lantern hanging over the front doors of the barn, and the dim light filtering in the window.

Jim Bond's hand closed on his gun. "No loud talk and no foolishness," he said. "If you start to act funny, I'll draw this time."

"Don't worry about me foolin' none," said Cole, looking at him keenly. "An' I meant it when I drew down on you up there. Now I'm glad Ed butted in. I reckon you're not here for your health." His words were weighted with a meaning Bond ignored.

"I don't have to go looking for something I've got," he said coldly. "If you've got anything to say, you better say it ahead of that mob you're traveling with."

Cole stepped quickly to the door and looked out. He turned on Bond with a bright light in his eyes.

"I'm not goin' to fool around with this," he said, speaking rapidly in a low, distinct voice. "You're here for something besides your health an' what the card tables would bring you, if anything. I'm all over bein' sore, not on account of anything you did, but . . . no matter. No man can work this place alone. You can take it from me that I know what I'm talkin' about. I'm takin' a chance talkin' with you at all. But I'm not so tied up that I'm not open to a proposition." He nodded significantly and again glanced out the door.

"I suppose your boss would be tickled stiff to hear that," Bond observed quite coolly.

Cole's face darkened. "Tell him," he shot through his teeth. "You can't get a crew in here, an', if you did, you'd have to fight him an' more others than you think. You can't do it alone, an' . . . you heard what I said."

Bond was frowning. "Who's this Porky?" he asked.

"A run-around for Tom Lester," Cole answered readily enough. "He was snoopin' around up there to . . ." He paused, listening.

Bond listened and could hear nothing. "Yes?" he prompted.

"Well, you can guess the rest," said Cole with a shrug, "but if you want to talk business with me, set a time an' place."

"Right here, one week from tonight," said Bond evenly. "And see to it that none of that bunch of cut-throats takes a liking to my horse. Understand?"

"I'll try to make it," said Cole, ignoring the reference to the horse. "An' I'm not worrying about you keepin' this to yourself, but it might be wiser. So long."

He left Bond more perplexed than he ever had been in his life. Bond had made the appointment on the spur of the moment, without reason and without any intention of keeping it. He had reminded Cole of the horse to avoid trouble, for if any attempt were made to steal it, he would have to act. Now he felt that the horse would not be molested. But he took no chances. He waited for an opportunity to speak to the liveryman, and, when he finally came, he told him straight.

"There's never been a hoss stolen in my barn yet, so keep your shirt on," the liveryman said gruffly.

Equipped with a legitimate excuse, Bond remained in the barn office. One by one the men rode out. Bond's thoughts were racing. Had Porky been up at the Farlin cabin hoping to steal money? Bond knew what the man's orders had been. He was to follow Farlin. Why was Farlin going away, and where was he going? And why was Lawson taking his outfit out of town on such short notice? Why was Big Tom Lester so interested in Farlin's movements? Bond could merely conjecture the answers to his questions, but one thing he knew—the queer business affected Gladys Farlin, and he wanted to help her. Therefore, he determined to take a hand in it. And no sooner had he made up his mind than he decided on a bold move.

He called the liveryman and ordered his horse saddled. Cole still was in the barn, and, when Bond left the office, Cole entered it. But Bond had no time for more talk with Lawson's henchman. He rode out of the barn and down the street, disappearing in the shadows of the trees as if he was riding eastward. He did not cross the creek, but tied his horse in the trees, and then made his way up the edge of the timber toward the Farlin cabin, where several lighted windows showed.

He took a position where he could see the front of the house and could hear if there should be any talking when the door was open. It was not his intention to wait long before ascertaining in some way if Lester still was in the cabin. He did not have to wait as long as he had expected. The door suddenly was opened and Lester's big form loomed against the beam of lamplight. Farlin's face showed over his shoulder.

"So long," said Lester, striding rapidly away.

"Good night," Farlin called after him, and closed the door.

Then Bond saw Gladys and her father facing each other in the square of light in a window. He forgot his decision to confront Lester as he saw the girl shaking her head and Dan Farlin putting his hands on her shoulders, nodding as he talked. Then the girl's back was to him and the gambler had disappeared. Bond looked after Lester, but the big man had vanished in the shadows down the slope. When he glanced back at the window, the square of light was vacant.

Bond was undecided, but now for the second time in the few minutes since he had arrived there he did not have long to ponder. The door opened and Farlin appeared. He had a coat on his arm. Then Bond saw the white dress of the girl and her arms about her father's neck.

"I wish you wouldn't go, Daddy," she said in a voice that convinced Bond she was close to tears.

"We've gone all over that," said Farlin kindly. "Now, do you promise?"

"I promise to stop you from taking chances, Daddy," was the answer.

Farlin kissed her, patted her shoulder, and then started down the trail, leaving her in the doorway.

Bond waited until the gambler was gone and the door had closed. He stood still, staring at the cabin, his brain whirling with the memory of Gladys' beauty as she had lingered in the doorway with the moonlight on her face. Then he swore mildly and softly, and finally stole around to the rear of the cabin and tapped on a window where a light glowed behind a curtain.

There was no response, and the cabin was silent. Then came a light sound on his right, and he whirled, to see the girl standing there with the moonlight glinting on her gun.

She lowered the weapon slowly. "What do you want now?" she asked in a slow, dull voice, heavy with worry, Bond thought.

"I told you, you might need a friend," he said, "and I'm here."

She looked at him a long time and her eyes suddenly filled with tears. Bond waited for no more. He took a quick step and gathered her in his arms, and held her while she sobbed softly.

Chapter Ten

Swiftly Gladys recovered and drew away with a quick look around. She put away the gun and dried her eyes with a diminutive handkerchief.

"That wasn't like me," she said. "But you might as well come in a minute. I don't expect Father back . . . right away."

She led the way to the end of the cabin where there was a small closed-in porch, and a door into the kitchen. The housekeeper stared as the girl and Bond brushed past her and entered the living room. There Gladys paused by the table, resting one hand upon it and gazing at him doubtfully.

"I don't know you," she said slowly, "but I've just got to trust someone, I suppose, and it might as well be a stranger as one of the crowd that hangs around this town."

"That's me," said Bond, nodding, with a sparkling light in his eyes. "You can trust me. I believe I told you that. I haven't sprouted any wings, and don't figure I ever will, but I'm not what you could call right out-and-out bad. I want to be the best friend you've got. I've made up my mind as to that."

Something in his voice and look caused her to turn her gaze aside.

"What do you suppose Porky was doing here tonight?" she asked.

"I think he came here intending to steal anything he could get his hands on in the way of money," replied Bond readily. "I happen to know he had an undesirable job on hand, and I think he wanted to beat it but didn't have anything to beat it on."

"He knows Father often has large sums of cash here," said Gladys. "He pulled the picture away from the wall safe, for one thing, and looked in the drawers. He didn't expect me home so soon."

"Then I was right," said Bond, nodding in satisfaction.

"Is . . . is he dead?" the girl faltered.

"No, and I don't think he's hard enough hit to die. That was brave of you to try to take the blame, Miss Gladys. But you might know I wouldn't let you do that." He smiled brightly.

"If you're the man they think you are, you don't need anyone to take the blame for anything you do," she said slowly, looking at him intently.

"Meaning just what, Miss Gladys?" he blandly asked.

"Are you Bovert?" she countered quickly.

"I'm Jim Bond," he replied. "Who's this Bovert?"

The girl shrugged. "He's a killer and all-around bad," she answered, not once taking her eyes from his. "He's bad enough for the sheriff to drift in here with word that he was on his way and to leave him alone. Guess he doesn't want any more trouble out this way than he can help. Lester and even Dad think you're Bovert, and . . . I'm wondering myself."

"All right," Bond said, his eyes flashing. "If I am Bovert, I'm bad. I'll leave it to you to figure out just how bad I am. But it takes a bad one to play with this bunch. I'm not counting your dad in on everything, understand. And this is all between you and me. We're getting acquainted fast. Suppose you just know me as Jim Bond, and forget the last name when you're talking to me."

"You don't seem to be very much afraid of this bunch," Gladys observed. "There was murder in Red Cole's eyes twice tonight. How . . . what kind of a job did Porky have to do that he didn't like, if it's all right for me to ask?"

"Lester told him to follow your father, find out where he went and what he went for, if he could," said Bond. "Lester seems to be interested in what your father does."

The girl's eyes flashed. "Of course!" she exclaimed. "He's afraid Father will leave town for good. He knows Dad is a drawing card for his place and . . ." She bit her lip in apparent vexation.

Bond put his hat on the table and stepped closer to her. "Now, Miss Gladys, it's time we talked frank and true. I've overheard a thing or two, but I'm just guessing. If you want me to help you, it's up to you to come clean . . . to tell me what you think is up. I'll shoot square and leave it to you to believe that my promise is good or not. But you've seen enough to know that I'm not in with anyone here."

"I suppose not," said the girl in a worried tone. "Well, I'll take a chance. Father does want to leave here, and he wants to take me with him and . . . and I want to go. He has bought a big ranch in Texas. He has business to attend to before he can go, and that's what is bothering me, because I don't know what it is, and he won't tell me. Lester doesn't want him to go. I'm afraid that Lawson has some kind of a big play on, and that Dad's going in with him. He's after a big stake, and it would be like him to take a big risk to get it. Now you have the substance of what I know, or don't know."

"And that's plenty," said Jim Bond enthusiastically. "Now you and me can put two and two together and get our bearings."

"You'll have to do the rest of the guessing," said Gladys wearily.

"And it's my guess that you're right"—Bond nodded—"but you haven't gone far enough." He looked at her thoughtfully. He was thinking of Red Cole's indirect offer to go in with him on a job, which Cole thought Bond also had in mind. So Cole must see the handwriting on the wall, too. Bond smiled broadly.

"If Lawson is planning a big job, he figures on leaving the country, also," he told the girl. "And Lester, maybe, is afraid he'll lose both your dad and Lawson's outfit into the bargain. Lawson and his bunch are good for a lot of money when they start spending. It's a three-cornered affair, and I'm going to play it that way . . . from your father's corner." He took up his hat.

Gladys hurriedly put a hand on his arm. "You mustn't . . . I mean you must be careful. What're you going to do now?"

"I'm going to follow your dad myself," Bond announced. "The thing for you to do is to get that Smith girl to stay with you while he's away, and, outside of that, go on with your work just the same as if nothing was up." He stepped toward the doorway leading into the kitchen. "You better have the light put out so I can slip out quick and sly," he cautioned. "And then . . . don't worry."

His smile reassured the girl and she called to the housekeeper.

"Don't take any big risk yourself," she whispered as he left her.

Jim Bond went out with a thrill tingling within him, and the next instant he was alert and stealing through the shadows toward the spot where he had left his horse. He now sensed why Cole had accosted him at the roulette wheel. He understood Lester's interest in him and Farlin's evident desire to play safe, although the gambler undoubtedly had thought to lower him in Gladys's estimation by playing on his suspected identity. As Bovert, he constituted a menace, as Jim Bond, he might easily be got rid of—perhaps. The part that he did not understand was the sheriff's warning to leave him alone if he should be Bovert. Meanwhile, how were they to decide? By putting him to the test.

These thoughts were racing through Bond's mind as he came to his horse. He untied the reins and had his left foot in the stirrup when a sharp command broke the stillness.

"Don't get on that horse."

Bond's foot came down in the instant his hand was reaching for the saddle horn to mount. He was caught fairly, and turned to see a big form looming in the shadow behind a gun that glinted in the starlight.

"An' don't move much," came the order. "Keep your right hand up in plain sight."

"All right, Lester," said Bond, recognizing the voice. "And you're kind of at a disadvantage in this light, are you not?"

"Not so much," said Big Tom with a short laugh. He stepped close to Bond and slipped his gun into its holster with a quick movement. "I'm willing to take a chance that I can shoot as quick as you can draw. This was the quickest way to stop you without startin' a fuss an' making a noise. It won't do you any good to draw now."

Bond glanced about quickly, trying to pierce the darkness in the trees.

"Don't worry," said Lester. "There's nobody here but me."

"Then you were taking more chances than you thought," Bond snapped, drawing his gun. "Now it doesn't make much difference if there's anyone around or not."

"I couldn't talk to you in the shop," said Lester, "so I waited till your visit to the young lady was over. I knew you'd go back up there, an' I don't blame you."

"That last remark wasn't necessary," said Bond. "You seem to be a busy man." His words implied a sneer.

"I reckon Dan Farlin would be less pleased than ever, if he knew Bovert was sneakin' visits to his daughter behind his back," said Lester, his words heavy with meaning.

"No doubt," Bond agreed. "This Bovert is bad medicine, I understand. Does he visit Farlin's place when Farlin knows it?"

Lester started to laugh again, but cut his simulated hilarity short.

"Never mind," he said in a patronizing tone. "I know you said your name was Bond, an' that's all right with me. I'm not telling what I know to anybody but you." He paused, and his listener knew he was bluffing. "I take it you're not up here on a vacation."

Bond started. It was the same intimation that had been made by Red Cole. Were two sides of the triangle trying to use him? He determined to learn what he could.

"I'm not old enough to take a vacation," he said, dropping the reins from his left hand.

"Of course not . . . an' that was just an opening." There were assurance and confidence in Lester's voice. "I've got a proposition. I don't know what you've got in mind to pull up here, an' I don't care." He paused to clear his throat and Bond immediately decided that this last was sheer bravado.

"I'll pay you well," Big Tom went on. "Porky went up to Farlin's tonight to steal some money. You caught him at it an' put him out for keeps. I had him in mind for another job. He wanted to beat it, for his nerve was gone. You can do the business, if you will, an' it'll give you an edge on Farlin in the bargain."

"I didn't put Porky out for keeps," said Bond, frowning.

"He's too old . . . he won't pull out of it," said Lester.

"Because you don't want him to, eh? You're pretty lowdown, Lester. I wouldn't finish the job on Porky, if I were you, and that's putting it to you straight. I mean it. That poor chap didn't have a chance with you. And you want to hand his job to me."

"I'd hand you a different job than I'd care to hand him," growled Lester. "I'm not afraid of you, Bov—. . . I mean Bond. If you was to have real trouble with me, it would only hurt any game you've got in mind up here. You've got sense enough to see that."

"Maybe you're right," said Bond, thinking fast. "What have you got in mind for me to do?"

Big Tom stepped closer and lowered his voice. "Dan Farlin is goin' out of town. He's goin' soon. Follow him, find out where he goes, an' why, if you can, an' let me know. I'll slip you a couple thousand, maybe five, an' let you in on something if you want it. An' I won't ask any questions."

Bond stood still, staring at him in amazement. Either the man was a plain fool, or he had some dangerous ulterior motive. Bond decided the latter was the case.

"All right," he said, "but suppose I run into Lawson's bunch? Cole has me on his list, you know."

"Cole an' the rest of them, except Lawson, left town a few minutes ago, ridin' west," said Lester. "Lawson is stayin' over, but you're not likely to run into him. Of course, you may have to take a chance or two, but I guess that ain't out of your line."

"No, I reckon not," said Bond vaguely.

"Then why . . . ?" Lester stopped and listened. The sound of a horse's flying hoofs came to them clearly from the trail leading east out of town.

"I . . . that must be Farlin startin'," said Lester, excited.

"In that case, I'll slide along after him," said Bond. "But there's one thing, Lester. Keep the wolves away from the Farlin cabin, and let Porky get well by himself. Is it a part of the bargain or not? If not . . . I don't go."

"It's a part," said Lester eagerly. "Go ahead, an' don't fall down on me, for I . . ."

But Bond had swung into the saddle and was riding in the shadow of the trees toward the east trail that crossed the plain to Crazy Butte and swung off to Rocky Point.

Chapter Eleven

When Jim Bond swung out upon the plain, he descried the lone rider ahead, a floating shadow on the prairie. He did not think that Farlin would ride fast, for he had shown the effects of the short ride he had taken when he had found Bond and Gladys together. As Bond's horse was fleet and possessed of great endurance, he felt he would have no difficulty in keeping Farlin in sight if he delayed his start. And, he was not altogether sure that the man ahead was Farlin.

Bond turned down along the trees on the bank of the creek and soon swung back into the shadows. He walked his horse back through the timber and tied it for the second time that night. He had seen no indication that he was being watched and was ready with the explanation that he wished to be sure that the lone rider was Farlin in the event that he was accosted the second time. He crept along the shadows to the rear of the Red Arrow.

During the short time he had been in the resort, Bond had been careful to inspect it thoroughly. He knew there were no windows in the side on which were located the bar, Big Tom Lester's private office, and the private card rooms. He knew, too, that only a thin partition separated Lester's office from the first of the card rooms.

He entered the rear door boldly, realizing that boldness rather than stealth would serve him best if detected. The narrow passage at the rear was deserted, but Bond heard the clicking of chips in one of the rooms. He made his way without hesitation to the room behind the office, opened the door, and stepped into its darkened interior.

Closing the door after him, he listened intently. He heard the low intonation of voices on the other side of the partition between the room and Lester's office. He snapped a match into flame and stepped softly to the partition and pressed his ear against it. He could make out Lester's voice and that of Lawson but could not distinguish what was being said. Finally Lester raised his voice in what Bond surmised was the end of the conference.

"He's following Farlin, an' I'm goin' in to Rocky Point tomorrow myself," was what he heard the resort proprietor say.

A chair scraped on the floor. "You're crazy!" It was Lawson who spoke, and his tone was angry. "If you want my opinion, I'll tell you flat that Dan's gone to town to stick a wad in the bank. He's mixed up in a ranch, so you say, an' he's got that girl of his to look after, an' why wouldn't he want to play safe?"

"I suppose you know that he rode out an' some way managed to meet this Bovert," Lester retorted hotly. "An' Bovert's already in sweet with the girl. Looks queer to me."

"If you think that way, wasn't it a wise trick to send this fellow after him?" sneered Lawson. "Do you think he's gone? All you did was to tell him what you was guessing. How you ever got where you are with all the mistakes you make is a mystery."

"I've sort of had you behind me," Lester blurted. "I know you wouldn't knock this place off after . . . well, we've helped each other. But Farlin's got something up his sleeve an' . . . to tell you the truth, I don't think for a minute that this fresh upstart is Bovert at all."

"An' that's right where you may be wrong," said Lawson. "Oh, don't look at me that way. I don't know any more than you do about him, but I'm not tellin' anybody what's goin' on in the back of my head."

"How long are you stayin' in town?" Lester demanded.

"I don't know," was the answer. "Where's that blunderer, Porky?"

"The doctor took him to the hotel, they say, an' . . ."

The voices died away as the office door was opened and the pair went out into the big room.

Bond now had need for caution. It was necessary that he get out of the place unseen. With Lester apparently planning to follow Farlin himself, and Lawson giving no reason for staying in Sunrise, and refusing to say how long he intended to remain, the indications pointed to a change of scene. Bond preferred to watch developments from the outside. He had no intention of letting any of the principals in the drama know of his presence in Rocky Point, in the event that the scene shifted there.

As Bond thought and listened, and finally became convinced that Lester and Lawson had left both the office and the station at the head of the long counter, he lit a match and stepped softly to the door. He waved the match out and put an ear to the panel.

At the moment he put his hand on the knob it was twisted from his grasp and a form burst in upon him. He staggered back and quickly leaped to one side of the door, dropping to one knee as a needle of fire cut the darkness.

Bond's gun came into his hand naturally, but he did not reply to the shot. Other forms were in the doorway, but they drew back. The corridor was but dimly lighted and Bond took a desperate chance, deciding upon the move, and making it, almost before the echo of the bullet's explosion died away.

He sprang out the door, shouting: "He's there! Watch out!"

Three or four men sprang back as a second shot roared inside the room and a bullet whistled past them. It was the man who had fired first, taking a chance of hitting Bond as he plunged through the door, and he had missed his quarry and narrowly missed hitting one of his companions.

For Bond it was the best thing that could have happened. He had got past the men, who, confused, believing him to be their companion, and expecting more shots from the room, had broken away. Bond sped around in the corner to the rear door in a twinkling. In another moment he was outside and dashing for the protecting shadow of the trees. Fireflies of death winked behind him before he reached cover in safety. He sped toward the place where his horse was waiting. There were no more shots behind him, and no shouts or sounds of pursuit. If Lester had suspected his presence in the room, or had learned of it through someone watching, he evidently had given orders to confine operations to the resort itself.

But these conjectures did not satisfy Bond in the least. If Lester had been sincere at first in sending him to follow Farlin, he had decided to double-cross him later, and, if he had engineered the attack upon him, he was throwing discretion to the winds. The thing that interested Bond was the possibility that Lawson might have been behind the attack. For Lawson was playing an under-cover game, even with Lester, possibly with Farlin and Red Cole, too.

A sweet party, Bond thought grimly to himself. *Maybe I'm dumb, but it sure looks like I've stepped into something.*

He stopped near his mount and listened with a frown, while his eyes searched the shadows as the dim starlight filtered down through the trees. This time he was not so sure of an ambush, and not at all certain of getting off in the event that there was one. As a last resort, those against him could easily disable his horse and leave him afoot at a dangerous time. There were two other points of great importance. If he were pursued, his followers would have a better chance to outwit him before he could reach Rocky Point, and there was also the probability—possibility, at least—that they might look for him at the Farlin cabin and perhaps molest Gladys. This last bothered him more by far than the other.

As he considered this, a horseman galloped below him on the trail to the east. Either Lawson or Lester was riding out of town.

This decided him, and he again stole up the slope to where he had a view of the Farlin cabin. No one was in sight and only two windows showed light. One was the window of the living room, and the other was the window of the kitchen, as Bond knew, being now partly familiar with the arrangement of the cabin.

He wanted to attract Gladys's attention and give her a word of further warning, but he hesitated to do so lest the place should prove to be watched. For one wild moment he considered returning to the Red Arrow, and, if Lester were there, shooting it out with him to destroy one angle of the triangle. He was young, filled with the spirit of adventure, perhaps—in love. The possibility had not entered his thoughts. Thus, the more he considered this step, the more he was tempted to yield to the impulse.

And then his next move was solved for him when two girlish figures came up the trail and he recognized Gladys and her friend, Louise Smith. They were talking rapidly in low tones and Bond waited until they had gone into the cabin. Soon another light shone and he surmised they had gone into Gladys's room.

He turned and retraced his steps through the deep shadow, proceeding with all the stealth born of his trail experience. In his absence a second horseman might have ridden east. He waited some little time near his horse and then went forward swiftly, untied the animal, and was in the saddle in the briefest space of time, swinging into the open and into the trail. When he had crossed the creek, he spurred his mount and soon was galloping on the open plain on the hard trail leading to Crazy Butte and Rocky Point.

He rode as fast as he could and had covered something more than three miles when the unexpected happened. The creek that flowed through Sunrise described a wide curve to the southeast when it left the town behind, whereas the trail led straight and true toward the east. The plain was a vast field of shadows but fairly lighted by moon and stars. Bond had good visibility ahead, and an attack from his left, behind, or in front, could easily be outridden. But now a rider came from the timber on his right, from the great bend of the creek. The horseman was speeding to cut him off, and left Bond the alternatives of veering to the north on his left, turning back, or attempting to outride the man who was racing from the south, on his right.

Bond chose the last alternative and called on his horse for a spurt to test the qualities of his pursuer's mount. The fact that but one man was following him led him to believe this was the man who had left town some time before. Surely Lawson would not think him fool enough to accept Lester's mission—if the outlaw believed him to be other than an adventurer—and Bond decided the rider must be Lester. It might be Lawson, but . . .

Jim Bond abandoned conjectures with a toss of his head and put himself to the task of riding his best, of getting all speed possible out of his mount, and the fine animal responded with a burst of going that soon put the approaching rider out of the running, so far as any cutting off was concerned.

In a matter of moments, the enemy changed his tactics, straightened out, and raced east in the same direction Bond was taking. The flowing plain with its billowing shadows became a racetrack, a straightaway with life for one or the other as the stake. Bond had no fear of his opponent, he had faced a blazing gun more than once, but in this instance he had no desire to take a chance of losing, because sincerely he wanted to do Gladys Farlin a favor.

Bond felt a wild sense of exultation as he gradually forged ahead, although he seemed to acquire his lead a scant foot at a time. However, unless the other rider was holding back, he had demonstrated to his own satisfaction that he possessed the better horse. Indeed, it would take a super horse, almost, to outdistance Bond's mount.

Bond now changed his own tactics. He eased his pace until he had fallen a bit behind. If the other wished to renew the spurt and fight it out, this was his opportunity. But Bond had no intention of spending his horse in a wild race on the open plain with a long way to go. This was wisdom, and the other apparently appreciated the fact, or realized he would be beaten, for he, too, eased off and gave up the effort. Bond again checked his speed until his horse was running at a pace he could sustain, if need be, for hours. The other did likewise. But both were making most excellent time.

Bond's expression had changed to one of grim resolve. Only a man accustomed to long hours in the saddle, to emergency speed contests, to hard, fast, exceedingly expert riding could put on the exhibition he had just witnessed. And Lester, keeping close to his place of business, engaged indoors at all hours, could hardly be expected capable of such a performance. The man must be Lawson.

The moon was riding into the western sky, and the light of the stars was dimming. The bulky form and jagged outlines of Crazy Butte were marching toward them. Dawn would not be long in coming. Jim Bond was not as familiar with this section of the north range as he could wish. He knew that the district around the butte afforded excellent cover, but the ride on to Rocky Point would have to be made in daylight. His pursuer would be at less advantage in broad day. If Bond could make the tumbled country around the butte in sufficient time ahead of his follower, he could hide out for a time, rest his horse, and move on to Rocky Point in the morning, in full view, riding his best and trusting to his horse—and to his gun if necessary.

The other must have been thinking much the same. He quickened his pace, and the real race was on.

Jim Bond fairly booted his horse ahead and rode him hard into the lead. Straight ahead, neck and neck, with his pursuer trying to maintain the pace and to draw closer at the same time. To attempt to shoot at the distance that separated them would be sheer folly. Bond laughed and raced for the butte, increasing his lead rapidly. Gray light streamed across the plain. The rider behind him suddenly slowed his pace and quickly drew far behind.

Bond shouted jubilantly and sped on. His adversary—Lawson, doubtless—had not the slightest wish to be recognized.

Chapter Twelve

Meanwhile, Dan Farlin had ridden even faster than he had anticipated. He had a good start on Jim Bond, to begin with, and considerable time had elapsed while events were in progress in Sunrise. As a consequence, neither Bond nor the mysterious rider caught as much as a glimpse of him as he proceeded swiftly on his way. Indeed, in the excitement of the race, Bond had forgotten all about Farlin.

The gambler reached the point south of the butte where the trail turned southeast for Rocky Point in due season, and at dawn was well on his way toward the county seat. There were ranches where he could have stopped, and at any of which he would have been welcome, but he preferred to push on. He was not riding on physical endurance alone, for his mind was busy with a hundred and one thoughts, suspicions, and conjectures. And out of this tangle came the conviction that he had to go through with the business in hand as speedily as possible. For Gladys, to all appearances, was altogether too much impressed by the young adventurer who he believed to be none other than Bovert.

And still he had inwardly to confess that Jim Bond, as the young adventurer called himself, had made a favorable impression on him. Damn it! What with a $100,000 ranch that he might never be able to pay for, a good-looking, vivacious, impressionable daughter, his own fondness—innate and studiously cultivated through the years—for games of chance, Lester's hold over him, and Lawson's proposition—he had much to think about. He did not look with favor upon the dubious role he was about to play, but—if he didn't do it, somebody else would. It was an old alibi for him.

He reached Rocky Point shortly after noon and, after putting up his horse, took the small pack from his saddle and proceeded to the hotel. His eyes glistened as he looked up and down the busy principal street. There was money in this, the liveliest town on the north range. It was supported by a rich ranching country and by the mining activities in the south. He thought it peculiar that Lawson had not made a raid here before, regardless of the "hands-off" agreement he had with Sheriff Mills. In fact, the immunity enjoyed by Sunrise was due in a great part to this agreement. And now the outlaw intended to make the long-delayed raid. It was brought home to Farlin with startling force that this was to be Lawson's final play in that territory. It was also to be Farlin's last hand thereabouts. With the agreement broken, what would happen to Sunrise—and to Lester? The gambler smiled grimly. Sunrise was doomed. And if Lester was to get an inkling of what was in prospect! The smile faded and the gambler's eyes hardened.

Dan Farlin was known personally to a favored few in Rocky Point. One of these was the proprietor of the leading hotel, the Palace. This stocky, ruddy-faced, good-natured individual spotted him as soon as he entered the hotel lobby and advanced with outstretched hand.

"'Lo, Dan," he greeted. "In so soon? Don't usually see you till after the Fourth. How's Gladys getting on these days?"

"Very well," said Farlin, shaking hands. "If I'm ahead of time, it's because things are slow and I thought a trip to the big town would do me good." His smile was engaging.

The proprietor became confidential. "If you're looking for a play here, Dan, you've come at the right time. Shearing's just over, the mines are booming, and there's all kinds of loose money hunting a new owner, and I can put you right. You're one gambler who can work this town and nobody'd kick."

Farlin laughed. "I never work any town, my friend," he replied with a suspicious twinkle in his eye.

"I know," said the other, raising his eyes. "You don't want the girlie in here, and I don't blame you. She's better off in Sunrise. This place"—he lowered his tone—"is getting tough."

"You don't say," said Farlin, feigning astonishment. "And just when was it that it got soft? I wish you'd have let me know, because I'd have moved in, bought a house, and planted a flower garden. I always loved flowers, old horse thief."

"Yeah? On somebody's grave who . . . oh, I didn't mean that, Dan. My jokes have a way of coming out twisted. At that, I've seen you wear a flower in your coat lapel, which is something I've never seen anyone else do around this burg. Now I know just what you want. You want a room, and you want a bath. And you're going to get 'em is what I mean. And when you're ready I want you to come down and have dinner with me. I haven't eaten yet, and I'll see the cook tosses up something you want. Come along."

An hour or so later, bathed, shaved, dressed as usual in his dark double-breasted suit, with white shirt and dark-blue tie, his boots peeping forth brilliantly polished, his diamonds flashing, Dan Farlin stood looking out the window of his room on the second floor, facing the street. A smart, splendid figure of a man—the most striking in that town. No one knew how he had come by his taste for sartorial perfection, for quiet, elegant dress. They assumed it was inherited. The big diamonds? They were expected of him.

Farlin's fine, handsome face was gathered in a frown. His talk with George Reed, the proprietor of the hotel, had disturbed him. Here was a man—a friend—who respected him. There were others. And Farlin did not pick his friends among the riff-raff of the cow towns and mining camps. And here he was about to— but they might never even suspect the part he had played with Lawson. He shrugged and went down to his dinner with Reed.

"You know, Dan," Reed said, when they lighted their smokes after the meal, "I've been wondering if you've ever thought of . . . of quitting the game you're in. Now, don't think I'm trying to butt into your private affairs, for I'm not. After all, I'm your friend. But Gladys is getting to be quite a girl, and you've got to think of her."

Farlin immediately saw an opportunity for an excuse if he should leave the country at all soon.

"I've thought of it, George. I've saved some money, and I'm going into ranching. No, not around here. I've a place picked out where the environment will be better for the girl. I think . . . I'm pretty sure I have enough to swing it. Now I'm going over to the bank and stick in a deposit."

He smiled as he realized for the first time that no one would suspect him of anything when they learned he had put money into the bank himself. As Lawson had craftily pointed out, he was in the clear and under cover.

"Good!" exclaimed Reed in satisfaction, patting him on the shoulder as they rose from the table. "And if you ever need, well . . . you know."

Again that queer feeling assailed Farlin, and he bit his lip. "I've got to go to the bank, George," he said hurriedly. "So long."

* * * * *

President John Duggan, of the Rocky Point State Bank, looked up with genuine pleasure; in fact, his large, genial face and blue eyes glowed as the immaculate gambler was shown into his private office—a new office, as was the cage before it. The interior of the old, trusted bank had been remodeled during the preceding winter.

"Dan, I'm glad to see you," he said, giving Farlin's hand a squeeze that made the latter wince. "Sit down in one of our new chairs." He indicated a chair opposite his big, flat-topped desk.

"I was just about to say that the place looks pretty high-toned," drawled Farlin. "New cage and floor and plate-glass windows, and then this office . . . and having to be led in. Guess you must have raised the limit on your interest rates, eh?"

"Nope," said Duggan, not without a note of pride. "We've always made money, and I, that is, the directors . . . ahem! . . . decided the building needed freshening up a bit. Country's booming around here and we have to put up a front."

"New vault, too?" said Farlin casually.

"Not at all. The one we've had right along is still large enough to hold all the money, but I'm hoping we have to enlarge it soon. You're looking good, Dan."

"Fishing for me to say you look the same," Farlin complained. "That's the trouble with you bankers. You always hem and haw and beat around the bush and make small medicine until you've got an idea what a man has come for. Then, if he's come to borrow money, your jaw drops a foot, and times are not good, and the outlook is doubtful, and there's signs of drought, and there isn't any too much water, and the grass is bad, and you shake your head and sigh and growl . . . 'How much yah want and what's the security?' But if he's come to put money into the bank, instead of take it out, why, then it's a case of . . . 'Ain't the weather good? Looks like one of the best years we've ever had. This is an excellent time to invest . . . right in this here country!' And you slap the desk and beam until one would think there were three suns shining instead of one. Now, how have you got me pegged? What do you think I've come for, John Duggan?"

The banker eased his huge bulk—he was a very big man—in his chair, leaned back, and laughed heartily. He wiped his eyes before he spoke.

"Doesn't make a particle of difference, Dan. If you've come to borrow money, you can have it. Not from the bank, understand. I have to account to my directors and . . ."

He was interrupted by Farlin's guffaw. "You and your directors!" said the gambler scornfully. "Say, John, if one of those directors . . . if you have any . . . came in here and said anything, you'd throw him out, and you know it."

"Tut-tut." Duggan frowned. "I'd be able to manage a loan, perhaps, but I'd have to guarantee it, that is . . . I'd have to be responsible for it."

"Now you're talking," said Farlin, waving aside the proffered cigar and taking out his tobacco and cigarette papers. "Well, John, I haven't come to borrow anything, except, maybe, a match. I've come to stick twenty thousand in that old vault of yours and just dropped in to say hello for the sake of politeness."

"By golly, things must have started off with a bang in your . . . your . . . ah . . . business." The banker smiled.

"Why don't you say what's in your head?" suggested Farlin. "Mine isn't a business, it's a game, and a rocky one at that."

"I wish you'd get out of it," said Duggan thoughtfully. "But right this minute, I don't know just what you'd do to . . . to . . ." He pursed his lips.

"To make as much money," Farlin supplied, smiling wryly.

"I don't believe you have any balance with us, Dan, but I'm glad to reopen the account. I'm mighty glad to reopen the account. And with no thought of the bank, I wish you'd keep a respectable balance for your own sake. Maybe you'll come out all right on your ranch deal down there, but cash is a nice thing to be able to lay your hands on when you need it quick."

"Have you told anybody about that deal?" asked Farlin quickly.

"Of course not!" Duggan exclaimed in indignation. "What I know . . ."

"Yes, yes," said Farlin with a wave of his hand. "You're just like a lawyer . . . and I wouldn't trust a lawyer so far."

"Say, Dan"—the banker leaned forward—"what does Big Tom Lester do with all his money?"

"I don't know," Farlin replied, surprised. "Hasn't he got any in here?"

"He . . . I couldn't tell you that," said Duggan. "It wouldn't be ethical."

Dan Farlin laughed. He was looking curiously about. There was a window at the rear of the office, and none too securely barred, he thought. The vault was the same and could be easily cracked. He felt that he was looking guilty when he again gazed at the banker.

But John Duggan was not looking at him. He was drumming on the top of his desk and staring through the open door into the cage. He turned his head suddenly.

"You know, it's too bad about that town of Sunrise," he said seriously. "It's in such a good location. And they're going to open up a big bunch of land north and west of there. This fall, maybe, next spring, sure. The government, I mean."

"Homesteaders!" snorted Farlin, unable to suppress a sneer.

The banker nodded. "They've got to come, Dan. There's no stopping 'em. It means farming country, and big ranchers will find that their land is too valuable to run stock on. When the time arrives, there'll be no kick from that quarter. Now, I'll make out your deposit slip myself and give you a book and a . . ."

"Don't need a book or receipt or anything," Farlin interrupted. He tossed the roll Lawson had given him on the desk. "There's twenty thousand there to start." He rose to avoid Duggan's eyes. "By the way, my daughter has an account here, hasn't she?"

"Yes." Duggan smiled. "I can tell you that because you're her father, but I can't tell you her balance."

Farlin frowned. Gladys would have to withdraw her balance before . . .

"Well, I don't want to know," he said. "So long, John."

John Duggan rose, stepped with him to the door. "I don't do this for everybody, Dan." He chuckled. "And everybody doesn't get in to see the president, either." His broad face beamed.

"John, we're both gamesters." Farlin laughed as he went out.

He looked about the rear out of the corners of his eyes as he left, and again the uncomfortable feeling swept over him. He was glad to gain the open air.

Chapter Thirteen

After the race to Crazy Butte, which he won handily, Jim Bond moved to the south, watered his horse, refreshed himself, and then climbed a ridge that afforded him an excellent view of the country to the east, south, and west. To his surprise, the lone rider who had challenged him had disappeared. Bond decided he had struck directly south into the screen of timber.

It was now broad daylight, with the sun climbing out of a sea of crimson in the east. The plain trail to Rocky Point was a gray ribbon leading southeast. There was no telltale streamer of dust spiraling upon it. For Farlin had passed out of sight in that direction and the lone horseman had not had time to reach it. Bond loosened his saddle cinch and permitted his horse to graze, while he sat down with his back to a friendly rock covered with moss and proceeded leisurely to roll and light a cigarette. The town that was his goal was off somewhere in the southeast, and, though he never had been there, it could not be such a great distance away. If it served the purpose of his pursuer to permit him to take the lead in the ride to Rocky Point, he was prepared to do so shortly. And, after the swift ride from Sunrise and the final, mad spurt, he entertained no fear of being overtaken.

Bond smoked contentedly. He now felt reasonably sure that Farlin had gone on into town, or that he was well on his way there. He had seen him start in this direction, and there was no other town within a great radius of miles to go to. And the gambler had made no preparations for a longer ride. Lester had as much as said he was headed for Rocky Point.

While he was smoking and resting, Bond kept a sharp lookout in all directions, as well as about the ridge where he maintained his vigil, and his ears were alert to the slightest sound. The sun emerged from the crimson banners on the horizon's rim and began its climb in the clear eastern sky. Black dots were visible on the flowing plain of green where cattle grazed. It was a quiet scene of solitary splendor and more than once the youth's thoughts flew back to Gladys Farlin in the wicked town in its setting of beauty, where the benchlands marched up to the foothills of the Rockies in the west. Youth and dawn and a universe of green, with a cool breeze playing, and a subtle, faint perfume as evasive as the movement of the atmosphere—boundless life, and joyous.

Bond stamped out the light in the end of his second smoke and rose quickly. He stretched his six feet of height luxuriously. Then he caught up his horse and tightened the cinch.

"If that *hombre* is waiting for us to start, horse, we're on our way," he said softly. Before he mounted, he drew his gun and examined it carefully, sliding it back and forth on his right palm, balancing it, and then whipping it back into its sheath with a move so fast that it might have been the lightning work of a machine.

He rode down the ridge on its east side where the small trees were far apart, and, in no time at all, so to speak, was on the trail that led straight across the rolling plain into the hazy southeast. He looked behind constantly and held his pace to a sharp lope. But there were no signs of pursuit. He decided that his follower was content to let him go on ahead, and he turned his whole attention to the business of getting into town as quickly as possible without calling upon his mount's reserve of speed.

The dust raised by Farlin's horse was hardly laid when Bond rode into Rocky Point.

By the simple expedient of massaging the liveryman's palm with a silver dollar, Bond learned that "his friend," Dan Farlin, had preceded him by a matter, almost, of minutes. He put up his own horse, carried his pack into the barn office, and made a few changes in his attire—after having used plenty of water and soap—and then avoided the gambler by going to a café to eat instead of to the hotel.

So Lester did not believe him to be the notorious Bovert, eh? At least, he had told Lawson that. Bond thought he had been lying. It did not require any great amount of sleuthing to hang around and witness Farlin's visit to the bank. His next move, for the bad man he was reputed to be, was a queer one. He secured his directions and proceeded straight to the county jail, which was a squat, square, stone building on a side street, graciously shaded from the hot rays of the sun by several big cottonwoods.

Sheriff Mills glanced casually from his newspaper to his visitor and took his feet from his desk as a token of respect and nodded in greeting.

"You the sheriff?" drawled Bond.

The official put down his paper with another nod. "Yes, I'm Sheriff Mills," he confessed, as if unwilling to make the concession as to his identity. "You want to see me?"

"Well . . . yes," Bond admitted. "Do you want to see me?"

"I always want to see anybody that has business here," was the sheriff's reply as his bushy brows drew together.

"That's it." Bond nodded. "I don't know if I have any business here or not, to spill the juicy truth."

"Then what did you come for?" Mills demanded.

"They as much as told me up in Sunrise that you're looking for a man named Bovert," said Bond calmly.

"Well, what of it?" growled the sheriff, biting off the end of a black cigar and staring hard at his visitor.

"They seem to think I'm Bovert."

"Well, are you? And whether you are or not, you can sit down."

Bond accepted the invitation. "If I'm Bovert, you ought to know," he evaded. "And if I am this gent, what do you want me for?"

"Who thinks you're Bovert?" the sheriff parried.

Bond tipped back his hat and sighed. "I guess you remember when I rode in on my way to Sunrise the other morning. Dan Farlin and you came prancing along when I was asking directions of Gladys . . . of Farlin's daughter who I happened to meet up with out there east of town. He seemed peeved, and you rode on back here."

"Oh, yes." Mills displayed more interest. "Yes, I remember now. You said your name was . . . was . . . ?"

"Bond. Jim Bond," the youth put in impatiently. "You'll remember I told him my word was as good as my name, but it didn't seem to make much of a hit with him."

"That's right." Mills nodded. "Dan's queer sometimes."

"This whole business seems queer to me!" Bond exploded. "I drift into Sunrise quiet as a kitten and find you've got 'em all het up by telling 'em a bad one called Bovert is on his way there, and to lay off. That big bag of wind, Tom Lester, gets it into his head I'm this man-eater, and sicks one of Lawson's crowd on me to feel me out. He's got Farlin to thinking the same thing. For all I know, that cut-throat Lawson's got it in his head, too . . . and he's nothing to meet on a dark night."

"I see." The sheriff yawned. "You seen to be having a hard time of it." His look and tone changed. "Suppose I said you are Bovert, and slammed you into jail?" he exclaimed curtly.

"You'd have a lot to prove afterward," Bond said coolly.

"You seem mighty sure of yourself, almost too sure, I'd say," was the sheriff's rejoinder. "Maybe you're wondering if I've got any authority around these parts. Now you've busted in here and shot a lot of questions, so I'm going to shoot a few back. Get me?" There was no mistaking the official's seriousness, for the way he put it showed that he meant every word he said.

"It's all right with me," Bond retorted defiantly.

"What did you mean by saying that Lester sicked one of Lawson's men on you? Who was it, and what happened? That's number one."

"I'll have to pass your number one, Sheriff," Bond answered complacently. "Lester wanted to try me out to see if I was the man he thought, that's all. I'm not here to give out information. If I'm the man you think, and you've got anything on me and want to jug me, why, I guess I've got everything with me I need to go to jail. Here's my gun." The weapon was on the desk before his last word was out.

The sheriff looked at him steadily, chewing on his cigar. "Maybe you'll answer number two," he said less sternly. "Did you follow anybody into town?"

Bond hesitated, puckering his brows. "Yes," he replied finally.

Sheriff Mills looked vaguely about the office, and then again centered his eyes on Bond.

"That's fair enough," he decided aloud. "I saw Dan come in, and you showed up next, so I could have guessed it all by myself. Number three makes it harder. Did anybody follow you in?" His gaze was now keen.

"I . . . don't know." Bond was puzzled by the sheriff's manner. And he really did not know if the lone rider had followed him, or had preceded him, for that matter. He had a feeling that the man across the desk from him was getting more information than Bond was.

"*Humph*," grunted the sheriff.

A long silence ensued. The sheriff relit his cigar, puffed upon it violently until it was burning well, looked critically at the end, and stared out the window where the leaves of the trees stirred and whispered in the breath of wind. Jim Bond turned his hat about in his hands by the brim, looked at the sheriff with a frown, and then at the gun on the desk.

"You want that gun?" he demanded.

Mills looked at the gun as if he were seeing it for the first time. "Nope. I've got one of my own that suits me, and I can use it when I have to. Nice gun, though."

Bond cleared his throat, and, without taking his eyes from the official, retrieved the weapon and slipped it into its holster. It was as if he expected the sheriff to come to life with a quick move the instant he reached for the six-shooter.

Another silence.

"Suppose I said I *am* Bovert?" said Bond suddenly, his eyes narrowing ever so little.

"That's your business," was the exasperating reply.

Bond swore softly under his breath. "It begins to look as if I didn't have any business here in the first place . . . or now," he said, slamming on his hat.

"I take it your memory is average," said Mills. "If you'll stir it up a little, you'll remember I didn't send for you." He looked at his visitor coldly.

Bond rose and leaned one hand on the official's desk, looking down at him with a quizzical light in his eyes and a queer smile on his lips.

"Sheriff," he said slowly, "we've either told each other a lot, or nothing, but we've each learned something. I'm not exactly sure what you've learned, and I'm not going to ask you, because you wouldn't tell me if I did." He paused, and Mills nodded brightly. "But I'm going to tell you what I've learned," Bond went on, "and that is that you're a mighty slick article." He drew out his last words and emphasized each of them with a solemn nod.

"There was only one other man who told me that." The sheriff sighed. "And he's dead."

"Died a natural death, I suppose," said Bond sarcastically.

"All men die naturally," the sheriff observed dryly, picking up his paper. "Something inside 'em stops working and they die."

"Yes," snorted Bond in disgust. "They die. So long." He turned to go.

"Where you going from here?" the sheriff asked sharply.

"I'm going to get myself a pack of cards and play solitaire," Bond flung over his shoulder.

When he had gone, Sheriff Mills put aside his paper, opened a drawer, and took out a manila envelope. For some minutes he scanned its contents. Then he again was interrupted, this time rudely.

Chapter Fourteen

It was Big Tom Lester who stormed into Sheriff Mills's office some minutes after the departure of Jim Bond. The resort-keeper closed the door after him, a thing that Bond had not seen fit to do. Lester's face was red and he was puffing with exertion as he faced Mills, who had quietly replaced the contents of the manila envelope in their container and put the envelope in a drawer.

"Sheriff," blustered Lester, "I've always played square with you, an' I'm not side-steppin' anything this time, but you gave me an order . . ."

"I never gave you an order in my life . . . not straight out," the sheriff interrupted. His tone was different from that he had employed in talking with Bond. He sensed that Lester had not seen Bond and gave the latter a mental credit mark for having avoided a meeting.

"Well, we'll call it a tip," sneered Lester. "You've given me a tip now an' then, haven't you?" He wiped his face and brow with a large handkerchief. His clothes showed signs of travel.

"Let it go at that," Mills snapped out. "And put a checkrein on your voice, Tom. I'm not deaf."

Lester cooled a bit and sat down. "You came out to town an' put me wise that a gorilla by the name of Bovert was headed my way, remember? Of course . . . an' you said to lay off him. We can call it a tip, but between ourselves it was more than that." He took off his hat and scowled darkly, while the sheriff surveyed him coolly and somewhat curiously. "Well, this terror of the big an' open showed up on schedule an' opened his bag of tricks *pronto* . . . an' in my place to boot!"

"You've got that kind of a place, haven't you?" the sheriff asked sharply.

Lester stared and opened his mouth foolishly. "Why . . . I've always had the same kind of a place . . . I . . . it ain't been so bad," he stammered.

"Well, they haven't held any services there for the common good that I've heard of," the sheriff shot back.

Lester's face darkened, and then he abruptly changed his method of approach.

"All right," he said, lowering his voice. "I don't claim to have any kind of a place except the kind I've got, although I haven't bothered anyone, either." He nodded at the sheriff, who nodded in turn. Apparently a more amiable understanding had been arrived at without the need of verbal explanation.

"This Bovert arrives an' first off picks a fight with Red Cole at a wheel," Lester continued.

"Picked out a tough one to start with," was Mills's comment. "What did Cole do to him."

"Well, he probably . . . he would have killed him, I reckon, if I hadn't given him the signal to lay off," replied Lester, rubbing his palms. The lie was written all over his face, but Mills merely smiled.

"So then," Lester went on, "he gets into trouble with my man, Porky, an' that was worse."

"Porky bored him, maybe," said the sheriff, who now seemed but mildly interested.

"No, he bored Porky," Lester flared. "An' I had to butt in again or Red Cole would have certainly put him away for keeps."

"Why, I thought Porky was such a bad man," the sheriff observed in mild surprise.

"He is a bad man!" Lester exploded. "But you told me yourself what a terror this Bovert was. I suppose you think Porky should stand up with him, especially when he doesn't give Porky a chance. I'd have gone at him myself if it hadn't been that . . ."

"That you was afraid of him," Mills interrupted, nodding.

Lester's face purpled. "We'll let all this go," he snarled. "The thing is that I'm not goin' to have him around there, bustin' up games an' raising trouble, an', if you want him, you can have him, but he's not safe in Sunrise any more. I came all the way here to tell you that I can't go through with my promise to protect him, that's all."

"I didn't ask you to protect him," said Mills coldly. "I said to lay off him, yes. I didn't want any trouble starting out there, maybe. What does he look like?"

"Well, he's tall, not so old, but he's got a mean eye . . . you can tell him by his eye. Oh, it's Bovert, all right. He's quicker than greased lightnin' with his gun, too."

"Give you any name?" the official inquired casually.

"Calls himself by the name of Bond," said Lester with a grimace.

The sheriff sat up with an intense show of interest. "Bond?" he said, wrinkling his brow. "Jim Bond? Youngish sort of fellow?"

"That's him," Lester answered, looking puzzled.

"Why, he was just in here," said Mills. "Said he come from Sunrise, too. I've never seen Bovert myself. I didn't know it was him . . . don't know yet. Said he followed Dan Farlin in. Has Farlin and him had any trouble?" The official appeared greatly concerned.

Big Tom Lester was staring, open-mouthed. He started to speak and the words died on his tongue. "In . . . in here?" he managed to get out at last, as if he doubted his own ears.

"Right where you're sitting," was the answer. "Didn't you know he was in town? He must have come right ahead of you. Did you know Dan Farlin was coming to town?"

"No!" Lester spoke the truth, but he saw no need of telling the sheriff he had suspected as much. But Bovert—seeing the sheriff! "What did Bovert come to see you for?" he asked, his eyes narrowing with suspicion.

"He wanted to know if I wanted him," was the ready reply.

The sheriff coolly prepared and lighted another cigar, while Lester watched him with a new and menacing light in his eyes.

"Say, Sheriff"—Lester's voice carried a new note and he leaned forward with his hands on his knees—"this Bond may not be Bovert at all."

"I didn't arrest him," said Mills laconically.

"That's it." A grim smile played about Lester's cruel lips. "He might"—he lowered his voice so it barely carried to the ears of him for whom it was intended—"even be connected with the law."

Mills looked up quickly. "You think so? Better be careful how you jump at conclusions, Tom."

"He might," Lester continued in the same tone, "even be one of your own men." There was a significant pause. "You don't have to spy on me, Mills. An' so far as I know, there's no reason why you should spy on Lawson. He's playin' the game, although he hasn't a thing to do with me. Don't forget that. He drifts in with his crowd now an' then, spends a little money, lets his men get the cramps out of their legs, an' moves on . . . but never in this direction."

The sheriff had been thinking rapidly. So it was Red Cole, or Porky, one of the two, that Lester had used to bait the man who called himself Bond. Lester had told him much and he had read more between the words spoken by both the resortkeeper and Bond.

"What makes you think Bond might be a law agent?" The sheriff scowled. "I've got to know that, Tom."

"Because . . ." Lester hesitated. "Oh, well, because he was the next thing to caught tryin' to eavesdrop outside my office last night."

Sheriff Mills tossed back his head and laughed. "Tom . . . Tom . . . you're upset," he said, recovering himself with difficulty.

"Just because I gave you a tip about this Bovert, you've got yourself all worked up. You just can't stand anything mysterious, eh, Tom? Everything's got to be right out in plain sight with the sun shining on it, or in the dark with you holding a match on it, or you're thrown off your balance, isn't that so, Tom?"

"You're not talking very clever," said Lester grimly.

"What's Farlin doing in town?" the sheriff asked.

"I don't know, an' you're gettin' away from what I was talking about, an' it don't look good, Mills."

"What were you talking about?" growled the sheriff.

"About this Bovert, or Bond, or whoever he is, being the law."

"You know just as much about that as I do," said Mills evenly. "If he's the law, I don't know it any more than I'm sure he's this Bovert. But there's one thing I do know, Tom, and I want you to get this straight. If he is the law, he isn't working at whatever he may be doing for my office. I don't have to sneak in any outsider to help me with my business, and you ought to know that. Sometimes I think you're losing your grip."

Lester started. He had heard that so often it was assuming the nature of a prediction. And he knew Mills spoke nothing but the truth when the latter told him he had no outsider working for him.

He rose. "All right, Mills. I believe you. But this smart *hombre*, whoever he is, isn't safe from now on in Sunrise. I'm doin' the square thing by declaring myself."

"Just one thing more, Tom," said the sheriff sternly. "Whoever he is, leave him alone. This isn't a tip, as you call it. It's an order!"

Lester moistened his lips and clenched his palms. "I suppose I should stand still an' let him shoot me down, if he sees fit," he said harshly. "I suppose that . . ."

"You suppose nothing!" Mills broke in, rising from his chair. "If he starts something when he shouldn't, providing he goes back there, that's his look-out, but don't you start anything . . . understand?"

Lester's eyes were blazing with baffled fury. "I'm beginning to think I understand a lot!" he shot between clenched teeth.

"I'm not worrying about what you think, Tom!" Mills called after him as he went out.

* * * * *

Big Tom Lester slipped into the rear door of a resort and managed to attract the attention of an employee, who came at his bidding.

"I don't want to see anybody yet," he said hurriedly to the man, who evidently knew him and stood with an attentive ear. "Just bring me a bottle of the best in this room here so I can take a snort or two alone. I've had a hard ride an' want to rest an' think a minute or two by myself, see?"

A gold piece changed hands and the man "saw" at once, and hastened to carry out the order. When he returned, Lester was slumped in a chair in the private card room, his hat on the table, a dark frown on his face. He tossed another gold piece on the board.

"Take it out of that," he commanded, and waved the man out.

Big Tom poured himself a big drink and downed it with two gulps. Then he tipped up the pitcher of water the man had brought and drained half of it. He had not particularly wanted the drink of fiery liquor, but he had to have a legitimate excuse for being where he was.

Never in his life had Big Tom been more angry, and at one and the same time so puzzled. Bovert or Bond—whichever he was—had followed Dan Farlin to town. Lester had known that before Sheriff Mills had mentioned the fact. It had been Lester who had raced that race for the wilds of Crazy Butte in the van of the dawn. But why had his quarry gone to the sheriff's office, and why had he told him he had followed Farlin to Rocky Point? Had he told him anything more?

Lester twisted about in his chair, his face dark, his fists clenched, his lips twitching. Mills had lied to him! Everything pointed to it! Why—why —why? Lester grasped the bottle and poured himself another drink and tossed it off. Perhaps he was going crazy.

It took a third drink to steady him, and then he decided that Mills had come to the conclusion that any means he might use would be fair in a contest with Big Tom Lester, czar of Sunrise. The fact that, if Mills had openly declared war, he would have won, that Lester would take what he had and leave rather than run the risk of losing all made the matter all the more puzzling and ominous. Well, now that it was war, the question arose— should he run away from a gold mine—and the Red Arrow was a gold mine if ever there was one—or fight? And if it were to be war, would Lawson stand behind him?

Lester put a hand to his wet forehead and had recourse to the bottle. The drink fired his brain with an idea.

Bovert, or Bond, or whoever he was, was the cause of it all. The thing to do was to get rid of him first off and running, and then act according to the way the wind blew. Lester smiled in satisfaction—and dropped his glass.

The door had opened silently. Jim Bond entered, kicking it shut behind him. He advanced softly to the table.

"Don't try to draw, big boy," he purred, "this is a friendly little visit. Still . . . stand up!" His gun appeared like magic.

Big Tom stood up, his jaw dropping, elevating his hands.

In a trice, Bond had relieved him of his weapon. "Now," said Bond, in a low pleasant voice, "we can talk and effect a little settlement." He seated himself comfortably and took out tobacco and cigarette papers.

"Settlement?" said Lester with a blank look.

"Sure." Bond smiled. "I've finished your errand, Tommy. I've found out where Farlin went and what for he went. Isn't that what you wanted me to do?"

Big Tom Lester dropped limply into his chair.

Chapter Fifteen

Sitting opposite Big Tom Lester, Jim Bond slowly rolled his cigarette with one hand, exercising meticulous care as to its symmetry, wetting the edge of the paper delicately, sealing it perfectly, pinching the end precisely, and then lighting it with a graceful movement of the flame of the match, looking at him the while with a cynical smile that maddened the trapped resortkeeper.

Wafting a smoke ring across the table, he said: "I've found out everything you wanted to know, big boy, so there was no need of you chasing out here." He nodded affably. He knew, or was very sure, that it was Lester, after all, who had raced him across the plain. He had seen Lester enter the sheriff's office but had been careful not to be seen himself. He had viewed Lester's lathered horse in the livery. He had hurried back and shadowed him into the rear of the resort. Now he had him dead to rights, he knew, for Big Tom could not shout for help without making a fool of himself and without having to put forth an explanation, and he had been disarmed.

"I suppose you think I needed your services," sneered Big Tom.

"You said you did, and you got 'em," returned Bond. "Farlin is right in this town." He leaned back in mock triumph. "You see, I trailed him. I found him and learned why he came. You might never have got here in time, if that nag of yours can't mosey along any better than it did this morning."

The flush in Lester's face was a dead give-away.

"So I finished the first part of Porky's job that you turned over to me," Bond continued. "Now for the second part. Farlin came here to pay a visit to the bank. I glanced in the window and he was in the back office. So I trailed in, made a deposit, and saw him toss a big wad of bills on the banker's desk. There! He came to Rocky Point, and he came to put some money in the bank. Now you have it. Only, I wouldn't let Farlin see me in town, if I were you."

Lester suspected this was a half truth, but he could not prove it. He started to speak and reached for the bottle instead—he needed a bracer, this time.

"So now," Bond continued cheerfully, flipping the ash from his cigarette, "we'll settle."

"Settle!" Lester ejaculated. "Settle for something I did . . . practically did myself? I chased you here, didn't I? You couldn't help yourself, could you? Settle for what?"

Bond's cigarette spun in the air on the instant. "Settle with me for doing your dirty work," he said, his eyes looking through slits formed by his narrowed lids. "Don't try to cross me, Lester. I'll make you crawl in the dust of the main street and put six slugs of lead in you in the bargain, or . . . I'll put one slug in you right here. Which do you want?"

Lester looked into the black eye of Bond's gun and gulped.

"How much do you want?" he asked in a gurgling voice.

"That's better," said Bond. "You must have some brains, and you never had a better chance to use 'em. You said you'd give me a couple of thousand to find out where Farlin went. I found out. You said, if I found out what he went for, you'd maybe make it five. I found out why he came here, and there's going to be no maybe about it. You're coming across with five thousand dollars, here and now, or you're going out of here on your hands and knees, or feet first. You can take your choice, big boy, and I'm not waiting long."

Big Tom Lester had mixed with men on that range long enough to recognize a dangerous one when he saw him, and to see and sense when such a man meant exactly what he said. Here was no henchman of Mills. He knew instinctively that Bond did not represent the law. This made him all the more dangerous. And he was not a novice. Perhaps he was Bovert, after all, and the visit to Mills had been an audacious exhibition of sheer bravado. More than likely Mills was not sure of his man. Otherwise, why had the sheriff ordered hands off in his case? But the matter at hand was far from trifling.

"You know I don't carry any such amount of money on my person," he complained, sparring for time.

"Imagine," commented Bond scornfully. "Big Tom . . . *the* Big Tom . . . going around with small change in his pocket. What're you playing me for? Don't you think I know men of your stamp? Inside, way inside, you're yellow. Here!" He put Lester's gun in the center of the table and put his own at the left end of the table. "Now. Make a grab for it. You've got as good a chance as I have. Go for your gun."

But Lester had no intention of going for the gun so close to his hand. He knew the signs. Now he had an inspiration.

"You win," he said. "I've had too much to drink . . . even if you put my gun in my hand, I'd probably miss. An' I haven't ridden so fast an' so far in a long time, although I was a rider in my day." A sparkle came into his eyes, to be succeeded by a look of cunning as Bond took up the weapons.

"Suppose I give you a thousand now an' the other four when we get back," he suggested.

Bond laughed coldly. "Tom, you're not half . . . not a tenth as smart as I thought you were. I'm going to have that five thousand now and here. And I'm going to salt it in the bank so you can't frame anything on me to get it back, see? I wasn't born yesterday, nor the day before, and I wouldn't trust you the width of this table. What's more, big boy, as soon as you've forked over the dough, we've got another little matter to take up. So you better get this over with quick. There's no use in you playing a waiting game"—he shook his head earnestly—"for if anybody happens to drop into this room, it's just naturally going to be your hard luck."

Lester reached inside his coat, took out a wallet, and passed Bond a number of banknotes that totaled $5,000. His face was white and his lips were drawn in a fine, white line. His eyes were pinpoints of smoldering fire.

Bond counted and pocketed the money. Then he rested his elbows on the table, with his weapon at his right, and spoke in a low, serious voice.

"I know exactly what's in your mind this minute, big boy. You're thinking that cut-throat friend of yours, Lawson, will help you out in this. You might as well get that out of your head. Lawson is no fool, if you are. He isn't going to pick trouble with a go-getter who isn't meddling in his affairs for the sake of doing a favor for a man who has done nothing more than kowtow to him and take his money and his men's money. He doesn't care the snap of his finger for you. I'm ready and willing, and anxious, to tell you that in his presence. So get that out of your head. You'd better ride back slow-like, when it's cool, and let the wind fan your piece of brain a little."

Lester opened his mouth and closed it. This was Bovert!

"Now, what was that other little proposition you said you might have for me if I carried out this job successfully?" asked Bond after a pause.

"That was a bluff," snarled Lester. "You can't kick. You've got your money."

"Well, you're telling the truth, at last." Bond nodded. "And that's the wise thing to do with me. Just keep on telling it and play safe. What were you doing talking to his nibs, the sheriff?"

"What was you talkin' with him about?" flared Lester.

"That's a fair question." Bond smiled. "I went straight to headquarters to find out if I was wanted. I know what you think. You think I'm an *hombre* called Bovert. If I am, I'm bad, big boy, and don't forget that. I know the word the sheriff left with you . . . to lay off me, if I'm this obnoxious person. I gave him a chance . . . or he thought I did . . . to grab me if he wanted me. Well, you see me sitting here, don't you? I expect he told you about it, you being an old pal of his. Now then, what did you go for?"

Lester was all at sea. This frankness disturbed him. He decided to meet Bond on his own ground.

"I went to tell him that I couldn't promise you protection, that is, I . . . my promise to him was all off," he finished with a scowl. There was one point that also disturbed him. Bond had made no mention of the attack upon him in the resort the night he had listened in the little room near the office. He decided that, if Bond didn't bring the matter up, he wouldn't accuse him of eavesdropping. In any event, Big Tom was becoming rather bewildered by the fast and unexpected turn that his trip had taken.

"Imagine you giving me protection," said Bond with a grim smile. "You'd have shot me down this morning if you could have got close enough . . . and if I hadn't dropped you first. Where's Lawson?" The question came sharp and clear.

Lester's eyes widened, and he put a hand across his mouth. "Not so loud," he said. "I don't know, an' that's the truth. Do . . . do you know?" He put the query anxiously.

"Nope." Bond shook his head. "I'm not meddling with him, as long as he leaves me alone. Say, Lester, why are you so all-fired curious about Farlin's movements?"

"I paid you five thousand for your . . . your services," Lester answered. "It wasn't understood that I had to make any explanation."

"You've got me there," Bond agreed readily. "Only there's one thing you don't want to overlook, big boy. Dan Farlin is an old-timer. If he knew you were so keen to pry into his business, he wouldn't like it a little bit. If he knew you'd put a man on his trail, he'd be plumb mad. He isn't afraid of you, and he doesn't pack that little snub-nosed gun of his in his cuff as a bracelet, either." He paused to let this sink in and saw a worried look in the big man's eyes for a moment. "If you try any underhand tricks on me, big boy," he went on evenly, "I'm going to tell Dan Farlin just how the trouble started, see? You can't blame me. I'm one man, but you're trying to make me think that you're an army, and I'm taking you at your word." He rapped sharply on the top of the table with the muzzle of his gun.

Lester started to his feet, but sank back into his chair at a signal from Bond, who sheathed his gun, broke Lester's weapon, spilled the cartridges into his hand, put them in his pocket, and handed the empty gun to the resortkeeper.

The man who had served Lester came in.

"Bring a bottle of ginger ale," Bond ordered, and Lester nodded.

When the man had gone, Bond spoke quietly.

"When he brings it, throw it out the window, or drink it, and tell him anything you please. If it should ever be necessary, Dan Farlin can make him say that we were together in this room. So long, Tommy."

Jim Bond went out, closing the door softly behind him.

Chapter Sixteen

When Dan Farlin left the bank, he sauntered about town. He nodded to casual acquaintances often but stopped to converse with none. He ventured into side streets, but they always were situated on the side where the bank was located, and, as the jail and the resort where Lester had repaired to be discovered by Jim Bond, were on the opposite side of the main street, he didn't have a chance to observe either of them. Farlin was concerned with the rear approach to the bank and its proximity to the main trails leading north and west.

To all appearances, his business completed, he merely was killing time before starting back after the heat of the day. But, in reality, he was getting the lay of the land, taking in every point of vantage that could be utilized in such a raid as Lawson planned. And it is extremely doubtful if any of the outlaw leader's followers could have obtained so much valuable information in so short a time. Farlin had made up his mind that he would not make more than one visit to the town in the interest of his present enterprise. If he could avoid a second visit, so much the better.

At last his inspection was ended. Farlin walked up the main street, undoubtedly the most distinguished-appearing individual in town. Oblivious of the attention he was attracting, the gambler continued on with his thoughts. Many times he had considered entering the very game in which the notorious Lawson was engaged. He had been turned aside in this ambition, first because of the ease with which he reaped a harvest at the green-topped tables, and second because of his wife, Gladys's mother.

He was going to have to leave all this—the scene he loved—and forfeit, perhaps, the respect of the men who knew him well. He shrugged. It was all in the game. But in his heart of hearts, he knew this was not true.

The genuine warmth in the greetings of George Reed, the hotel proprietor, and John Duggan, the banker, lingered in his mind. It was also noteworthy that Farlin realized keenly that he took two risks—the risk of being identified with Lawson's nefarious undertaking and the dangerous prospect of being double-crossed by the outlaw. The news that the vast domain about Sunrise was soon to be developed ordained in advance the passing of that town as a rendezvous for the lawless. John Duggan might just as well have told him that the north range careers of Lawson, himself—yes, and of Lester—were soon to end.

Dan Farlin's fine eyes lost their luster in a glint of hardness. Since this was to be his last play, he would make it pay as no other game ever had paid him in the past. He would send Gladys away from the scene, and he would himself engineer and direct the raid upon the bank and . . . He stopped in his tracks with a new and startling thought. Perhaps Lawson already had considered the new angle, but—why not knock off Big Tom Lester's place in the bargain? Two big jobs, and two big splits, and independence on a big scale for the rest of his life, with Gladys well provided for when he should pass on.

The gambler's eyes gleamed; he straightened to his full height, and threw back his shoulders involuntarily. It was like calling "fours" with a "full hand" when he was not sure but that he was beaten. He started and turned almost guiltily as a familiar voice fell upon his ear.

"What do you think of the old town since we dressed her up?"

He looked into the quizzical, blue eyes of Sheriff Mills. His first thought was of the remodeled interior of the bank. "A few coats of fresh paint will do wonders, Sheriff," he replied at random. A sly glance about, however, showed him he was not far from the mark.

"Bet your life," said Sheriff Mills heartily. "I've been preaching the doctrine of fresh paint for years, and this spring, when the boom started, they got together and decided I was right. Did you see how they've fixed up the bank?"

"Couldn't miss it," said Farlin, looking the other squarely in the eyes. "Just stuck a wad in there for safekeeping in case I was to get old and need it."

"You'll get old one of these days, Dan," mused the sheriff. "And your game can't last forever, no matter how you play it."

Farlin frowned. "Say, Mills, are you going to read me a lecture?" he asked. "Because if you were figuring on doing that, you can save your breath. I've been reading myself a lecture these past two or three years. We're both old-timers, and I guess we can read the writing on the wall. And you're in a better fix than I am."

"So?" Mills seemed surprised. "Why, you must have quite a pile cached somewhere, Dan. You haven't been reckless here lately."

Farlin shrugged. "I only have one business, if you can call it that," he said cryptically.

"How's tricks out at Sunrise?" asked Mills casually.

"Hard to take," was Farlin's short answer.

"Anybody come in with you?" asked the sheriff absently.

"Not that I know of," replied the gambler with a sharp look.

Mills decided that Farlin did not know of the presence of Bond and Lester and made up his mind not to mention the coincidence of their being in town at the same time. Possibly there was no connection between their visits and that of Farlin. But he was thinking.

"Figuring on a little play here in town, Dan?" he asked.

Farlin smiled. "Once a gambler, always a gambler . . . eh, Mills? Suppose I was hankering to finger the pasteboards here,

Sheriff. Suppose I'd come to the conclusion that this was rich territory . . . then what?"

"No objection on my part," replied Mills readily enough. "You know I've never kicked on your play. Of course, I've never lost any money in a game that you were in," he quickly added as an afterthought.

Dan Farlin laughed outright, and, when Farlin laughed that way, it was good to hear. "Mills, I'm almost beginning to think you're a friend of mine," he said, sobering suddenly.

"Thinking back quite a spell, I can't remember ever having showed myself to be your enemy," drawled the official, squinting.

"That's three of 'em," Farlin muttered. He was thinking of Reed, Duggan, and the sheriff. "Nice of you to say that, Sheriff," he said. "And the enemies I've got stay pretty well under cover." The last words carried a grim note.

"Well, I haven't been to dinner even," said Mills, looking at his ponderous watch. "Do you calculate to go back soon, Dan?"

"I'm sleeping in town tonight," said Farlin. "I don't like to stay away from Gladys long, but I'm not the rider I used to be."

"Then maybe we'll meet up later," said Mills as he moved away.

Farlin looked after him. Of all the people on that range, none knew better than Dan Farlin what a smooth, shrewd man was the sheriff of Crazy Butte County. At this very moment, he knew Mills had something on his mind, and he sensed that it had something to do with Sunrise and the people there. Could it be possible that he had an inkling of Lawson's plan—perhaps even of Farlin's connection with it? The gambler thoughtfully resumed his walk.

Farlin dwelt, too, on the sheriff's question as to whether he was in town alone. For the first time he considered the possibility of having been followed, but he put this aside with a shrug. What difference would it make? Only one man—Lester, possibly—could be interested in his movements, excepting Lawson.

Anything that Lester could learn as to where he had gone would avail him nothing, and Lawson could not come to Rocky Point without breaking his truce with Sheriff Mills. Besides he . . .

The gambler yawned and went to his room in the hotel. He had no intention of remaining there all night, but there was no reason why he shouldn't take a nap and start back in the coolness of the early night. He was downright tired, and the weakening reaction of the nervous strain he had been under had set in. He turned in for forty winks as he promised himself.

Meanwhile, Jim Bond did go to the bank and deposit the $5,000 that Lester had paid him, and more besides. He, too, snatched a light rest, but it was in the barn, for he intended to be the first to leave for Sunrise in the evening. Lester disappeared from the scene entirely, put up in sleeping quarters, doubtless, by a friend in his own business. His trip to Rocky Point had availed him nothing, although he more than half believed all that Bond had told him. Thus it was a queer triangle of affairs in Rocky Point this afternoon.

When Dan Farlin woke, it was dark. He hastily lighted the lamp and found it was nearly midnight. He had overslept by hours! Moreover, he was stiff and sore as the result of his long ride. He bathed his aching body in hot water and dressed hurriedly. He went to a small café for something to eat and then repaired to the livery. He asked if anyone he knew had been in, but the night man did not know him and replied in the negative. Farlin did not bother putting any questions elsewhere and rode away shortly after midnight.

It was torture for the first two miles that Farlin rode, and then the soreness began to wear off and a feeling akin to exhilaration possessed him. It was a night made to order, as he himself expressed it. A great silver moon rode among the star clusters and a soft wind laved the land of weaving shadows. He had a good horse. He flattered himself that he was not old for his age. And he had Gladys. Surely if ever a man had a legitimate reason to turn such a trick as he contemplated, it was he. Three of them—Reed, Duggan, and Mills—and what good would they do him if he were down and out? A loan! For what? To be used as a stake to gamble himself into the money again! No, he had to go through with Lawson. But . . .

He had nearly reached the dividing of the trail south of the butte when a shadow, swift-moving, detached itself from the black hand of the trees and sped toward him.

Farlin instinctively reined in his horse, the Derringer sliding into his right hand, and waited. Long before the rider came up to him, he recognized the burly form of Lawson in the saddle. He sighed with relief and the deadly little gun disappeared.

Lawson held up a hand as he approached. "'Lo, Dan," he greeted genially. "I had to ride out this way an' thought you wouldn't mind if I trailed along with you."

"It's poor judgment," said Farlin coldly. "We may not be the only people riding about and it wouldn't look good for us to be seen together. I suppose you never thought of that." His last words were brimming with sarcasm and struck an antagonistic note in Lawson.

"You needn't be so particular," said the outlaw. "We're alone. I've had my eyes peeled, so don't worry."

"I suppose you were afraid I might overstay," said Farlin. He was nettled and suddenly the outlaw's presence was repulsive.

Lawson quieted his horse. "Listen, Dan," he said in an earnest voice, "I've been on your trail . . . keepin' out of sight, remember. I don't know if you know it or not, but two people followed you to town."

Farlin recalled instantly the sheriff's query as to whether he had come alone. "What of it?" he asked somewhat belligerently.

"Just this," replied Lawson sharply, "this isn't a kid's game we're playin', an' I'm not takin' any chances of bein' double-crossed myself and I'm not takin' any chances of you bein' double-crossed. Did you see anybody in town from Sunrise?"

"No," Farlin answered bluntly. He was not altogether at ease.

"Well, that Bovert or Bond . . . that young fellow who's been buttin' in on things generally . . . followed you in. Lester sent him. Lester told me himself that he sent him. An' then Lester, the big jackass, followed his man, tried to outrun him in a race to the butte, lost out, an' he went on into town. Now, you know something."

Dan Farlin was frowning. "Lester's afraid I'm going to quit his joint," he said, half to himself. "He's a fool."

"Sure," Lawson agreed. "But in messing around the wood-enhead's liable to get something into his nut that don't belong there, see? As for that young snort, Bond, I can attend to him fast enough."

Farlin started. "Leave him alone," he said shortly. "We don't want any rough stuff in this, Lawson."

"No?" Lawson's tone implied a sneer. "Well, I'll look after that end of it. This is a big play an' there's too much at stake to let any lumbering *hombre* like Lester, or any whippersnapper like Bond . . . no matter how tough he is . . . gum things up. See?"

Farlin looked about. The huge, black bulk of Crazy Butte rose above them in the north. To their left—eastward—were the dark shadows of the trees in the tumbled lands and southeastward the plain flowed in shadowy waves under the moonlit sky.

"Well, this is a fine open spot for a conference," he observed.

"Lester an' Bond have ridden back toward Sunrise," said the outlaw. "Bond went first . . . an' fast. Lester's takin' it easy. I've been on watch here ever since you went to town."

"All right," Farlin snapped out, "we might as well get down to cases in this thing."

"That's right," said Lawson eagerly. "What'd you find out in town? I could have gone in, understand, there's nothing I've got to be afraid of there. But I thought it would be better if I wasn't seen there. You know how it is. What do you know?"

"Plenty," replied Farlin shortly. "I've got the lay-down pat. I don't know as I would have to go in again at all if it wasn't for a bit of personal business that has nothing to do with this deal, or you. By the way, I deposited that twenty thousand in my name, of course."

Lawson chuckled. "Of course, of course. But it would have given that old fogy of a John Duggan something to think about if you had used my name. I heard they'd made some changes in the bank. Is that so?"

"I know all about the changes and everything else," said the gambler. "I know everything. And I'm not spilling a thing until the time comes. There's one thing we've got to understand, Ed. I'm not in this business through any love for you or respect for your game. I'm in it for the money. Don't get me wrong as to why I'm throwing in with you. When this thing is over, I hope I never see you again. That's how much I think of you personally."

"An' I don't care a whoop what you think of me!" Lawson ejaculated. "Although I always have had a likin' for you, Dan," he added hastily. "But you haven't made the money you should. You say we've got to get down to cases. All right. This is my last play around here, an' . . . unless you're a fool . . . it's yours. An' the beauty of it is that there's goin' to be just the two of us in the big money."

"That's why I'm going to watch you like a hawk, Ed," said Farlin grimly. "You'd shoot me in the back in the wink of an eye if you thought you could get away with all of it. Well, I'm going to see that you don't. This is the first job of the kind I've tackled. I'm engineering it, and I'm going to boss it. You can tend to the men and . . ."

"An' take the big risk!" sneered Lawson.

"While we've been talking, I've decided to take the big risk with you," Farlin announced calmly. "It's the only way I can play safe. Now, do we understand each other?"

Ed Lawson's angry look changed to one of admiration. "If I ever had any thought of double-crossin' you, Dan . . . which I hadn't . . . what you just said would drive it out of my head. What's more, I see your brains are goin' to count more than my guns in puttin' this raid across. I don't mean to leave the boys who have run with me flat, remember, but . . . an' I'm lookin' to you to keep this to yourself . . . when this job is wrapped up an' put away, I'm quittin' the gang an' the country. You can use your own judgment."

Farlin had listened carefully and now he smiled to himself. For all his seemingly straight talk, Lawson's words lacked absolute sincerity. It just wasn't in the outlaw's make-up to play square all the way.

"Well said," was Farlin's comment. "We won't talk any more tonight, Ed. We'll talk further in Sunrise, three . . . maybe four or five days from now. And it wouldn't be best for us to ride on in together," he added pointedly.

"I'm steerin' northwest to check up on the boys," said Lawson, scowling. "I'll come into town to see you . . . alone."

"So long, then," said Farlin.

They separated, with Lawson riding off north and Farlin proceeding on his way to Sunrise, where events already were shaping themselves in an astounding way he could not suspect.

Chapter Seventeen

Jim Bond did not oversleep. At an hour after sunset he had eaten and was in the saddle, having noted that Farlin's and Lester's horses still were in the livery. Having contributed generously to the liveryman's supply of ready cash to keep his own movements a secret, he rode fast and was unaware, of course, that he was observed by Ed Lawson when he swung west of the butte and struck out in a straight line for Sunrise. As yet Bond did not know all he wanted to know, but he thought he did know the reason for Dan Farlin's visit to Rocky Point, and he was satisfied that Sheriff Mills didn't want him for anything specific enough to arrest him, and was not sure as to his identity. He classed Lester as a fool who was afraid of losing Farlin for a drawing card to lure gamesters to his resort.

Bond rode hard, polishing off the miles at a swinging lope that his horse could easily maintain to Sunrise, with speed in reserve when needed. Bond had no intention of reaching town after either Farlin or Lester had arrived there, and he had no particular interest in anything that might take place in Rocky Point in the meantime. Dan Farlin, he knew, could take care of himself, and it was only with Farlin that he was concerned, with the gambler and his daughter Gladys.

By this time Jim Bond had made up his mind that his interest in Farlin's beautiful daughter was not a passing fancy. His was not an idle infatuation. He wanted to see more of her, to talk with her a lot, to hold her in his arms, yes—to own her. This was what he told himself with a thrill as he raced across the plain under the drifting moon and the swarming stars.

Bond had a definite plan that he had decided to put into operation as soon as he arrived in Sunrise. His movements might depend to some extent upon what had taken place there in his absence, provided Lawson had stayed there. He did not trust Lawson, for he knew the outlaw's breed. And, first of all, he wished to make sure that Gladys Farlin was safe. Later he might have something important to tell her. The very thought of being in her confidence gave him a thrill. It would serve to cement their—their friendship. Maybe it . . .

Jim Bond dreamed on under the stars and it is doubtful if ever a horseman covered the distance between Rocky Point and Sunrise in better time than that made by him this night, without straining his mount. First and last, Bond knew horses, knew his own especially, and was careful to ask of the animal only that which could reasonably be expected by a horseman of experience and consideration.

The pale light of dawn suffused the east when he rode into town. It did not take Bond long to learn that Lawson was not in town. Nor did it take him long to learn that Gladys Farlin was all right, although she had not sung the night before in the Red Arrow. He learned, too, that Porky Snyder was reported to be doing well and was in a room in the hotel. He was careful to whom he addressed his inquiries and he was treated with respect. It amused him to find out that his defiance of Red Cole had given him a reputation and that he was looked upon as a gun expert who it would be well to avoid.

Much of this he gleaned from the sleepy hotel clerk, and it was through him that he arranged to gain access to Porky Snyder's room, regardless of the doctor's instructions that the little gunman was not to be disturbed. It was broad daylight when he slipped into Porky's room.

The window shade was drawn and the light in the lamp was burning. Bond threw up the shade, extinguished the light, and turned to find Porky's eyes open, wide and staring. He looked pale and shrunken in the white bed. There were bottles of medicine on the dresser. Bond opened the window as high as it would go.

"How do you feel?" he asked, pulling a chair beside the bed.

"Good as I could expect," growled Porky in a faint voice.

Bond looked at him keenly. "You're coming along all right," he said confidently. "I got that from headquarters, but I can see it with my own eyes. Do you feel as if you could talk a minute?"

"What's it about?" said the sick man with a scowl.

"I'm sorry this thing had to happen, Porky," said Bond in an earnest, friendly tone. "You're old and wise enough to know that it was the only thing I could do. I could have bored you for keeps." He paused and frowned. "I'm sorry I said that, Porky. Now listen. I'm just back from Rocky Point. Of course you know Farlin went in. When you couldn't follow him like Lester wanted you to, he had the nerve to turn the job over to me. Then he followed me and tried to pot me. I made him cough up five thousand dollars, and I'm going to split with you. I'm not fooling for a quarter of a split second. I want you to know I'm on the square, and I'm the only one here who is on the square with you. Get that into your head and keep it there. Your supposed-to-be-friend Lester wanted to finish you."

The little gunman's eyes were popping and a slight flush came into his withered cheeks.

"You're . . . goin' . . . to . . . split?" he mumbled.

"Twenty-five hundred dollars is yours when you want it," Bond assured him. "And now I want you to do me a favor. So far as Lester is concerned, you're through. I guess you know that. So far as I can make out, you never did much good for yourself by trailing with him in the first place. I'm going to tell you a thing or two, Porky, and I'm going to trust you. I guarantee you a sweet piece of change if you play with me, and a new chance as well as a chance to get even with Lester. I called the turn on him in Rocky Point, and he's a rat. I want to know why he's so interested in what Farlin does, and what's going on under cover here. I rode hard to get back here and have this talk with you before Lester or Farlin could get back. And Lawson's no friend of yours, either." Bond leaned forward and tapped Porky on the arm. "I'm your best bet," he said convincingly.

But there was a flicker of suspicion in Porky's eyes. "What makes you so interested in all this?" he demanded in a stronger voice.

Bond smiled. "Here's where I have to trust you, Porky," he said in a low voice, smiling faintly. "It's Farlin I'm interested in. I don't want to see him get in bad in anything. You're no fool and you should be able to guess why I feel this way."

"They say you're dynamite," grunted Porky. "You got a job planned up here?"

"I didn't have. But now I guess I have."

The little gunfighter's eyes gleamed. "Farlin, eh?" he said in a whisper. "You want to keep him out of trouble because of the girl? Is that it, eh? Am I right?" He rose partly on an elbow.

"I knew you were smart enough to guess it." Bond nodded.

Porky's face froze into cold lines. "She's a nice girl," he said significantly.

"That's exactly why I'm interested, Porky," said Bond, and there was no mistaking the ring of truth in his voice.

Porky looked away. "That makes it different," he murmured. Then he smiled a bit wistfully as if the thought that he might be able to do a good turn was agreeable. Next he looked at Bond sharply. "You're sure?" he asked sternly.

"I don't have to answer that question," said Bond with a light frown. "You know I'm sure."

"Gimme a glass of water," Porky ordered. "An' if Lester or Lawson find out I told you, they'll fill me so full of holes that a hunk of Swiss cheese would look like a solid brick alongside of me." He drank the water in long gulps. "Now there's a nip of likker in that top drawer. Gimme that." The stuff caused him to gasp for breath, but he talked rapidly under its stimulation. "Lester's out of it," he told Bond. "All he's afraid of is that Dan Farlin will leave the town an' the Red Arrow'll lose a bunch what comes there just to play with Dan. Anyway, that's as much as I know. Of course, he would like to find out how much money Dan's got an' all that, an' he's jealous of him because he's so popular an' ain't afraid of him. He thought he had Dan under his thumb till Dan showed him a while ago that he was all wrong. Then he saw Dan an' Lawson with their heads together an' . . . well, Lester's always been the suspicious, sneakin' kind. You know?" He paused, and Bond nodded. So far, his own conjectures were right.

"The other mornin'," Porky went on, lowering his voice to a whisper so that Bond barely could hear, "Lester put me on Farlin's trail. Farlin went to breakfast with Lawson, an' I followed 'em. I took a big chance to overhear part of what they said in a booth at the café. I thought later on I could worm a bunch of money out of Lester for what I knew. Fat chance. " He sneered and asked for a cigarette.

Bond rolled a smoke and gave it to him. He knew better than to interrupt the gunman's trend of thought.

Porky took a few puffs, his gaze sharpened, and he leaned toward his listener.

"This whole thing around here is goin' to bust up," he said. "Lawson's goin' to beat it, an' Dan Farlin's goin' to beat it. Lawson's laid off of Rocky Point so's he'd be left alone when he breezed in here with his bunch. Now he wants to make a last big haul . . . the bank at Rocky Point." A weird grin played on the speaker's lips. "You begin to get it?" he asked in a tone of triumph. "He put it up to Farlin to throw in with him an' get the lay down at the Point. Lawson can't circulate down there without the sheriff gettin' wise to him an' everybody puttin' extra locks on their cash boxes. Farlin saw a chance for a big rake-off, an' he took it. He went to the Point to get the lay of the land for Lawson. Now you've got it." He leaned back, smiling.

Jim Bond took the deadly right hand of the gunman in his own. His eyes shone.

"Thanks, Porky," he said simply. "And remember that anything I do is because I know Gladys Farlin is a nice girl, as you put it. You and me are together in this and you can be sure that from now on you've got a two-fisted, hard-shooting, square friend in Sunrise. And I'm forgetting you told me a thing."

"Funny you didn't ask me why I was up to Farlin's cabin when I got shot," mused Porky with a curious side glance.

"I figured you were trying to cop a roll and beat it yourself," said Bond with a wave of his hand.

"You're not so dumb," Porky grunted. "Now get out of here before somebody shows up."

Bond left as unobtrusively as he had come.

Chapter Eighteen

To Porky Snyder's secret amusement and delight, his next visitor (he didn't take into account the man who brought his breakfast or the doctor) later in the morning was none other than Big Tom Lester.

The resortkeeper had shaved and otherwise erased the marks of travel, but fatigue showed in the intricate wrinkles about his eyes, and in the eyes themselves, although he strove valiantly to imbue them with a cheerful sparkle.

"Well, well, Porky, old-timer, they tell me you'll be on a sunfishin' bronc' in a few days," he said, rubbing his hands. "I'm mighty glad to hear it, 'cause I was worried. I'd have been up here sooner, but"—he looked swiftly about and lowered his voice—"when *you* couldn't go, I followed Farlin myself." He nodded energetically and took the chair near the bed. "How do you feel?" he asked with real concern in his voice.

"I'll pull out of it," replied Porky laconically with a queer look. It was like having a play enacted for his special benefit, and he with foreknowledge of the plot.

"Why, of course!" exclaimed Lester. "Does the doctor say how . . . how soon you'll be about again?"

"You know how those pill-mixers are," Porky complained. "They don't say anything. I reckon it's up to my constitution."

"Well, you've got that," said Lester in a satisfied tone. "Now, don't you get to feelin' down-hearted. I'm goin' to give you some money, even if you couldn't do the job I asked you to do. You don't have to worry about that. I was wonderin'." He hesitated

141

and then said: "What in thunder was you doin' up at Farlin's place?"

"Thought I might get some advance information," said Porky.

Lester indulged in a wry smile. He knew this was a lie but he had to accept the explanation. Porky had gone up there to crack Dan Farlin's strongbox and then he had intended to beat it. That was the size of it. Farlin must suspect that, too. Very well. Porky was more in Lester's power than ever and Lester intended to use him in a desperate way. And then—get rid of him.

The resortkeeper became even more confidential in manner and speech.

"Listen, Porky, what was that young fool of a Bond doin' up there?" he asked. "I'll tell you why I'm curious afterward."

Porky could have laughed in Lester's mean face.

"Why, he was tryin' to buzz around Farlin's girl, of course," he answered.

"Was he the one that shot you?" persisted Big Tom eagerly.

"Now you've got me," said Porky. "I don't know who shot me. I was all in a daze an' went out quick. I woke up here."

"I see." Lester nodded. It annoyed him to realize that he didn't know if Porky were telling him the truth or not. Still— what difference did it make who shot him? He shrugged as if he were dismissing the matter from his mind as unimportant. "All right. Now, Porky, old-timer, the thing for you to do is to get well as quick as you can. Do what the doctor says an' don't worry. I've got something good for you when you can get around again. This isn't a cheap job. It'll bring you in enough to keep you for more than one winter. Cheer up an' say nothing. Just leave it to me. An', by the way, send over for anything you want. I'm tellin' 'em downstairs that I'm responsible for all your bills, understand? They know you've been workin' for me off an' on an' won't think anything of it. I'm standin' right behind you, you know that, don't you?"

"I'm glad to hear it," said Porky. "I need a friend now."

"Well, you've got one in me just like you always had," Lester declared, rising. "If you want anything, just let me know. I'll be up to see you right along an' you just cheer up an' get back on your feet. See?"

"What kind of a job you got comin' up for me?" Porky asked. "I'm sick of this trailin' people around an' . . ."

"You don't have to do another bit of it," Lester broke in.

"Is . . . is it a killin' job?" Porky asked softly, his eyes holding Lester's.

"If it was, wouldn't I be a fool to say so ahead of time?" scoffed Lester. "Just you get well an' then we'll talk proper. You don't even have to tell anybody I was up here. You an' me must stick together, Porky. An' let me tell you one thing . . . this shootin' wasn't any half accident like some folks would have us believe. Don't forget that. I'm leaving this quart in case you need a nip." He took a bottle from inside his coat and put it in a drawer of the bureau. Then he took his departure.

If Big Tom Lester could have seen the look on Porky Snyder's face a few moments later, he would have been in no mood for the sleep he needed so much. For the little gunman's eyes gleamed with malice and hatred, contempt, and disbelief. He took his tobacco and papers and painfully managed to roll a cigarette. Lester was through!

* * * * *

Dan Farlin sat at supper in his cabin with his daughter Gladys. He had talked casually but to the point during the meal, answering her questions to her apparent satisfaction. Gladys had listened attentively, stealing keen glances at her father from time to time. "And so I've decided there's no use in finishing out the season here," he said, putting down his napkin with an air of finality. "This town is played out. John Duggan told me himself that the homesteaders were coming next spring. You know what that means. It means farmers, people of small means, if any, who will build shacks and fences, dig wells and haul coal, and plow, and what-not. They don't make live towns like this one and they're no good for my business." He lifted his brows and looked at his daughter.

"If they do come," said Gladys seriously, "they'll make this a livelier town than it ever was before and in a decent way."

"Now don't start that," said Dan Farlin sharply.

"I will start that," flared Gladys. "I'm sick and tired of all this. I suppose you and Lester and Lawson thought this country would stay wild and untamed forever."

"Don't link me with that pair," warned her father.

"Why not?" The girl looked surprised. "They're in the business, as you call it, are they not?"

Farlin shook his head impatiently. "Well, you're going to have your way," he said in resignation. "I'm going to quit and I'm going to move out. We'll go down to the ranch. But you needn't tell anyone about it . . . not even that Smith girl."

"When are we going, Daddy?" asked Gladys, brightening.

"Within two weeks, I hope. And we'll need all the ready cash we can get together. So if you've got any money in the bank at the Point, get a draft for it, or draw it . . . and soon."

"I'm willing to do that," said the girl. "I'll have it when we're ready to go."

"And there's a couple of other things." Her father frowned. "I wish you'd quit the Red Arrow and not sing there any more. I think Lester has guessed I'm figuring on leaving and he doesn't feel any too hilarious about it. I'd rather you wouldn't do your turn there from now on. I've quit splitting with him on my end."

"Just as you say, Daddy," Gladys assented.

"Then there's that young fellow who's been hanging around," Farlin went on. "He's stuck on you, of course. I don't blame him. Cut him out, Gladys. He's bad medicine. I've got that straight. You'll do that for me and for yourself, won't you?"

Gladys laughed. "If I'd string a sheepherder along, you would worry, wouldn't you, Daddy?" She got up, went around the table, and put her arms about his neck. "You know I can take care of myself, don't you, Daddy?"

"Yes," answered Farlin grimly. "But this bozo isn't one to be strung along. He's dangerous, dearie. It bothers me to have you even listening to him. It might have been lucky that he was around when Porky tried his little stunt, but . . ."

"Yes?" prompted Gladys.

"He had no business up here, just the same," growled Farlin.

"I suppose you want me to believe that he's this terrible man, Bovert, you've mentioned," the girl suggested.

"I happen to know," said Dan Farlin grimly, "that he is."

Gladys caught her breath sharply and turned away. Her father looked after her with satisfaction. And yet he liked the fellow.

* * * * *

Farlin walked down the trail into town in the last glow of the sunset. It would be interesting to meet Big Tom, since he knew the resortkeeper had followed him to Rocky Point. Dan Farlin was rather pleased to have something up his sleeve. It would be interesting, too, to see the young desperado who called himself Bond. Funny business—Lester hiring this Bond to do an errand for him and then trying to do for him on the open plain. Was Farlin as valuable to Lester as all that? And what, Farlin thought suddenly, did Bovert, or Bond, have up his sleeve? He didn't think too hard. The spring twilight was too beautiful with its pink and purple shadings. A cool breeze was blowing in from the open country. Birds were singing their nocturnal serenade in the arching cottonwoods. It was good to be alive. At forty-five, Handsome Dan had never felt younger. He found Big Tom, refreshed by sleep, at his place in his establishment and his face immediately broke into a smile. Big Tom seemed astonished at this show of cheerfulness and also somewhat taken aback.

"Hello, Tom," Farlin greeted cordially. "Guess you didn't expect me back so soon, eh?"

"Well . . . I didn't know," stammered the discomforted Lester.

"You don't seem any too glad to see me," Farlin observed.

"Oh, yes I am," said Lester hastily. "I was just surprised . . . well, to tell the truth, I didn't expect you back quite so soon."

Farlin laughed easily. After all, Lester was a great deal of an overgrown kid. "I just slipped into the Point, Tom, to put some money in the bank." Lester's start was not lost upon him. "I thought somebody might try to make a raid on my cache, but I never suspected your Man Friday would have the nerve."

"I've given Porky his marching orders," rasped Lester, scowling hard.

"Looks to me like our little stranger gave him his orders," Farlin remarked dryly. "Anyway, let us take just a wee libation, Tom. I hope we're still friends."

"We've never changed so far as I'm concerned," said the puzzled resortkeeper. "You're not figuring on quittin' us just yet, then?"

"I'm one of those men you can't put your finger on," said Farlin mysteriously. "My business isn't stationary like yours. And . . . oh, yes, Tom. I'd rather Gladys didn't do her turn down here for a while. You remember that cowpuncher that got fresh and I had to slam? Well, with this stranger hanging around . . . you know."

"I don't blame you," said Lester, eager to please. "Sure, it's all right with me if she stays away for a time. She's her own boss so far's I'm concerned, anyway. I've never tried to dictate to her . . . or you, either, Dan."

Farlin nodded soberly. Big Tom was not a novice at lying. "Speak of the devil," said Farlin, nodding toward the front of the room, "here he comes now."

Jim Bond strode jauntily down the bar. Lester's face went dark, but Farlin studied the handsome, debonair youth intently.

He held his head up and his eyes were everywhere, but not unpleasant. He radiated confidence. Yet he gave one the impression of nerves strung on a hair-trigger. He walked straight to the pair at the end of the polished bar. "Will you gentlemen take a light one with me?" he invited. And, without waiting for the nods in the affirmative, he turned on the man in the white coat. "Make me a tall, cool glass of lemonade," he said in a deep, agreeable voice. "Use one lemon and a spoonful of powdered sugar and shake it up with ice. And don't forget to strain out the seeds," he added, smiling.

"That," said Dan Farlin, "is to my certain knowledge the first glass of lemonade that was ever ordered over this bar."

"For a nickel I'd order it not served," snapped Lester.

Jim Bond spun a silver dollar on the bar so that it slowly moved in Lester's direction. "I haven't got a nickel," he said, looking the resortkeeper straight in the eyes. "Will a dollar do just as well?"

"We'll take the same," said Farlin quickly, clamping a hand on the spinning coin.

"That's all well and good," said Bond, still looking at the Red Arrow proprietor, "but I want this man to know that I order what I want, and I usually get it."

"You mean you're lookin' for trouble," said Lester hotly.

"Want me to change my order?" asked Bond coldly.

Lester's jaw clamped shut and at a nudge from Farlin he turned back into the office.

"Why start something here?" asked Dan Farlin sternly.

"To show you that he's yellow!" Bond retorted. Then he deliberately turned his back on the gambler and walked away.

Chapter Nineteen

Before Jim Bond could reach the door, Dan Farlin's hand was on his shoulder, whirling him about. Bond's right hand dropped to his gun but hung there as he looked into the gambler's eyes, hard and cold.

"Here's your dollar," said Farlin, holding out the coin Bond had spun on the bar. "I suppose you think I'm going to pay for the drinks you ordered. Is that it?"

Bond's eyes brightened. He took the dollar. "I'd plumb forgotten about that," he said. "I don't like to remember anything unpleasant. Do you still feel like drinking with me?"

Farlin stepped closer and his words were for Bond alone. "You made a crack down there about Lester, but don't get it into that fresh head of yours that I'm yellow. You've been playing a pretty high hand here. High hands happen to be my specialty. I'll draw cards with you any time, and I'm not particular who you are or what you are. We'll drink and you'll pay for it, of course."

"Of course," Bond agreed with a sparkle of admiration in his eyes. "And you can draw cards, like you say, with me any time. But I'm standing pat all the time. And that's an answer." He turned back to the bar with Farlin following, his brows creased.

"There's something I'm going to have to ask of you," said the gambler, toying with his glass when they had been served. "I'm asking you to stop annoying my daughter." His tone was quiet, but firm, and a stern look went with it.

"Has Miss Gladys complained?" asked Bond blandly.

"I am doing the complaining, understand?" replied Farlin.

"Sure." Bond nodded. "You've got me wrong, but we'll let it go at that." He lifted his glass of lemonade.

"I've got you right, if you want to know," Farlin snapped out. It was rarely he lost his temper, but the youth's complaisance exasperated him. Moreover, he wasn't at all sure that he did have this man right—which didn't serve to soothe his ruffled feelings. Bond appeared to be mocking him in a subtle, confident way.

"We'll let it go any way you wish," said Bond coldly. "And now, if it's jake with you, I'll shoot a hundred on the wheel."

The white-coated servitor took a liberty as Bond stepped to a roulette table.

"He's as smooth as they make 'em," he said to Dan Farlin in an undertone. "It's goin' to take a fast man to give him what he's lookin' for, believe me."

Farlin favored him with a look of contempt.

"Your brains just naturally run loose when you haven't got a hat on," was his comment. He stood against the bar and watched Bond win five stiff bets, pocket the money, and saunter out.

Bond strolled up the street and entered the general store. A man was lighting the hanging lamps and Bond waited until he was through. Then he bought some tobacco.

"Is Miss Smith around?" he asked casually. "Nothing important."

"Why . . . er . . . she's over in the post office," said the clerk who showed by his manner that he had heard things about this customer. He pointed to a booth at the lower end of the store and Bond saw Gladys Farlin's friend behind the window there.

"Thanks." He nodded, and strolled down to the post office.

"How do you do, Miss Smith," he said pleasantly. "Do you mind my speaking to you a moment?"

"That depends on what you want to speak about," replied the young lady primly. "You're a stranger to me."

Bond instantly formed a correct opinion of her.

"I'm not exactly a stranger to your friend, Gladys Farlin." He smiled.

"That has nothing to do with me," said Miss Smith stiffly.

"In that case, I beg your pardon," said Bond politely. "I'm sorry to have bothered you."

"Was it . . . anything in particular?" asked Miss Smith as he turned away.

"Why . . . yes . . . and no," he said in a hesitating voice. "I was going to ask you to do me a favor, but I guess I haven't the right."

"That would depend on the favor," the girl compromised.

"Well, you see, it's this way," said Bond, wrinkling his brows. "I want to get a message to Miss Farlin and I don't exactly think I should go up there. Well, I thought maybe you might be going up"—he lowered his voice to a confidential whisper that interested his listener mightily—"and I thought, if you were going up, you might . . . but I guess you wouldn't want to."

"Carry your message?" said Miss Smith a bit breathlessly.

"I had no right to think you would do that, Miss Smith."

Louise Smith had heard a thing or two about this dashing young stranger. What she had heard from her father—which was not so complimentary except as to Bond's expertness with his gun—had thrilled her. What she had heard from Gladys had puzzled her. But he was far too good-looking to be as bad as he was painted in some quarters, she decided. Besides, no one knew for sure. And maybe he was in love with Gladys. This thought also thrilled her.

"Well," she said, fussing purposelessly with some papers, "I am going up to see her, and I don't know why I shouldn't take your message, if . . . I don't see why it wouldn't be all right, do you?"

"Why, no," he replied with a smile. "It's just that I want to see her this evening. If she would walk down the trail after a while, Miss Smith, I'd be sure to see her and maybe she'd talk with me a minute. It really is important, in a way. Do you think she would come?" His tone was so humblingly anxious that Miss Smith decided on the instant.

"I'll tell her," she promised. "I wouldn't be surprised if she came. She isn't going to sing tonight. I'll tell her."

"Now that's kind of you, Miss Smith," he said with a note of mingled gratitude and enthusiasm in his voice. "I'm going to buy a nice box of candy right now . . . ."

"I never accept presents from strangers," she broke in severely.

" . . . for both you girls," he concluded with his flashing smile. "I . . . don't know any other girls up here and I hope you won't think it's a bribe. It'll make me feel good, anyway."

He took his leave of her, touching his hat brim, bought the candy, and instructed the clerk to give it to the young lady in the post office "for her courtesy"—which left the clerk in a perplexed mental torment.

Jim Bond was calmly deliberative during the next hour. He went to the livery to make sure that his horse was properly taken care of, and to speak casually with the night man in charge of the barn. He learned that Gladys Farlin hadn't ridden out as usual at sunset, that her horse had not been out of the barn from the time her father had left, that Lester's horse had been hard-ridden while Farlin's had been well-treated. He learned, too, and it gave him pause in his conjecturing, that Lawson had ridden out of town the same night Farlin, Lester, and he had left. None of Lawson's men was in town. The barn man showed interest in his questions and evinced a desire to please. For all of which he was paid in gold and put under promise to keep what Bond had asked to himself.

This was one of those beautiful nights of the prairie spring, with a scented breeze blowing and a big orange moon swimming in a field of stars. Bond loitered in the shadows about the trail to the Farlin cabin. Lights were burning up there. Would Gladys come? Everything seemed to hinge on her action this night. Bond looked up at the friendly moon and decided it was worth taking a long chance—as he was doing—in the desperate drama being enacted here to win her favor. Why not let Farlin go ahead with his plan to help Lawson rob the Rocky Point bank? What difference would it make to Bond how Farlin got his money, or what he did with it? And why not let Farlin go through with everything, then protect him against Lawson and hold his knowledge as a club over the gambler's head in his desire to win favor with Gladys? He spurned this thought almost from its inception. And he was rewarded by a vision of color that flitted through the trees from the cabin. Gladys Farlin was coming.

"I had to take this means of meeting you," he told her when she reached him, "because your father gave me my orders tonight, and I didn't want to run the risk of trouble . . . more trouble . . . by coming to the cabin. Your meeting me here means a lot to me, Miss Gladys."

"I couldn't help myself, I guess," said the girl anxiously. "Did you learn anything important?" Her eyes were wide as she looked up at him.

"Yes . . . but I'm not going to cause you any more worry by telling you what I know, or think I know," he replied.

"Do you think this is fair?" she flashed.

"I really think it is best," he returned. "I know what your suspicions are and there may be cause for them."

"Then Father is planning to do something with Lawson?"

"I want to put a question to you straight, Gladys," he said, placing his hands on her shoulders. "Would you want your dad to put in with Lawson on a last deal, even if you knew it would be successful and no harm would come to him?"

"No!" she exclaimed impulsively. "And Lawson would be sure to get the best of him in the end."

"Maybe you're right," said Bond. "But I'm going to butt in and stop anything like that. I don't want to preach any heroics, girlie, but why do you suppose I'm taking a hand in this?"

She looked up at him for some little time before answering. If this man really merited the sinister reputation that had been bestowed on him, he might be taking a hand in whatever was going on with a view to profiting for himself. Or was he bribing her in such an indirect fashion?

"I'm not sure," she answered him, looking away.

"That's just it," he said in a tremulous voice. "It's just what I thought. I wouldn't think of beating around the bush with you. Men don't usually step into danger . . ." He paused, and then: "We'll say men don't always take a long chance for charity or because they . . . I'll start all over by telling you, Gladys, that I like you. I like you enough so that it isn't just friendship. I know you love your dad. I like him myself, but I'm doing what I am, for you. Don't misunderstand me, for I'm putting my cards on the table. I want you to like me, even be grateful to me . . . anything so long as you don't dislike me. And to show you that I'm not trying to bribe myself into your favor I'm going through with this thing regardless of what you say or think."

Gladys was thrilled and his earnestness struck a responsive feeling within her. "I don't believe . . . everything they say about you," she said. "After all, I need a friend . . . a man friend . . . on my side."

"I don't care what you believe of what they say about me," he told her feelingly. "I just care about what you believe of what *I* say. I'm in love with you, girl, and now you have the whole story."

One of her arms went suddenly about his neck and he waited no more. He took her boldly in his arms and kissed her. And Gladys thrilled to the warm pressure of his lips. Gunman, killer, bandit, what-not—she returned his kiss.

"That's all, now," he said, releasing her. "You must trust me, and for your own sake and your dad's, you must obey any message I send to you. I'm leaving town for a day or two, but I'll be on hand when the time comes. I'm trusting you as I never trusted a girl before when I tell you that you can get word to me in an emergency through the last person you would think of . . . Porky Snyder."

She looked at him with shining eyes, and then turned abruptly to hurry back to the cabin.

Dan Farlin confronted her in the living room.

"Where have you been?" he demanded in a voice he never before had used in addressing her.

Gladys resented it instantly.

"I've been for a walk," she replied, tossing her head defiantly.

"You've been out meeting that fellow!" her father accused, his face darkening. "You needn't try to lie to me . . ."

"I've no intention of trying to lie to you," she broke in soberly. "But I'm of age in more ways than one and I can refuse to answer your questions. After all, a father can be a gentleman with his daughter."

Farlin's face had gone pale. His next words came through his teeth. "He isn't going to put over anything on me," he said grimly. "He's cooed to you until he's got you to liking him." Farlin was not displaying his usual strategy, or diplomacy.

"And what of it?" said the girl with another toss of her head.

Farlin's temper exploded. "Just *this*," he shot. "I'm going to kill him!" He slammed out the door.

A moment later, Gladys's clear ringing voice came from the porch. "Watch out, Jim Bond!"

An answering whistle came from below.

Dan Farlin swore, clamped his jaw shut, and went on down the trail to town.

Chapter Twenty

A silent spectator of the clandestine meeting between Jim Bond and Gladys Farlin had been Big Tom Lester. He had heard some of what had passed between Bond and Dan Farlin in their conversation earlier in the evening and he had anticipated Bond's next move. The resortkeeper had left his place of business by the rear door in time to see Bond on his way to keep his rendezvous with the girl. He had trailed him and had slipped away unobserved after the meeting. He was just entering his resort when he heard the girl's cry of warning and Bond's whistled answer.

Back in his cubbyhole of an office, Lester smiled to himself. He believed matters were working out to his advantage. It might be that Dan Farlin would try to put Bond away himself—and he might succeed. Farlin was no slouch with his Derringer and none could accuse him rightfully of lacking courage. Lester would have shot Bond down from ambush, but the sheriff's warning held him back, and down in his heart he lacked the nerve. For Bond had been right when he had formed the opinion that Lester possessed a yellow streak.

But, while Lester recognized Farlin's courage and his skill with his weapon, he overlooked the fact that the gambler reasoned calmly and coolly in such an emergency after the outburst of white-hot anger. Therefore he was somewhat disappointed when Farlin came into the place shortly afterward, the same debonair gambler as of old. Certainly there was nothing in Farlin's look or manner to indicate that he had any murderous intentions.

Lester, annoyed by Farlin's complaisance, decided upon a bold move, hoping that Farlin might inadvertently let something slip.

"Say, Dan," he said confidingly, "maybe I know something that would interest you."

"It wouldn't surprise me any if you did," Farlin observed.

"The only thing is"—Lester regarded him doubtfully—"you might think I was buttin' in on your personal business."

"It wouldn't be the first time," was Farlin's cheerful comment.

"Well, I think you ought to know." Lester frowned. "I don't see how I'd be shootin' square with you if I didn't tell you what I saw tonight."

Farlin favored him with a sharp look. "Your eyes always are open, aren't they, Tom," he observed.

"They have to be in this game," Lester retorted crossly.

"I've often wondered why you didn't get out of it, Tom."

Lester's frown deepened into a scowl.

"I've got too much at stake," he snapped, "an' nobody knows it better than you, Dan. What's more I don't want anything to happen that would sour you on the town. Not just for business reasons, but because I like you."

"Of course." Farlin nodded. "That's understood, Tom."

"Well, anyway, this young upstart who's been galloping around here of late is gettin' fresher every minute. An' what do you think I saw tonight? I happened to go out by the back way an' I saw him sneaking in the trees. For all I know the fool may figure on tryin' to take this place. I followed him to see what he was up to an' I saw . . . I saw . . ."

"You saw Gladys meet him," Farlin supplied disdainfully.

"So you knew it," said Lester, puzzled. "Well, I sure was surprised an' you can't blame me for thinking I should tell you."

"And then, I suppose, you heard Gladys call something to him?" Farlin suggested pleasantly.

"Why . . . yes," stammered the flustered resortkeeper who felt uneasy under the gambler's steady gaze.

"Just so," said Farlin coldly. "Now you just forget all this and let me tend to those personal affairs you mentioned."

"It's none of my business." The frustrated Lester shrugged.

"And that's the proper way to look at it." Farlin nodded. It was odd to stand listening to the confidences of the man whose every secret move he knew, thanks to Lawson and Porky. "Did you hear any of the . . . ah . . . conversation, by any chance."

"I wasn't close enough," growled Lester. "But I saw plenty."

"No doubt . . . only you've forgotten what you saw," Farlin warned.

"There's a bunch in that want a big game tonight," said Big Tom, changing the subject. "Do you want some of it?"

"Sure," replied Farlin genially. "I'm on."

* * * * *

Jim Bond had seen things, almost in the wink of an eye after his meeting with Gladys. He had caught a glimpse of Big Tom Lester, stealing back into his resort by the rear door and suspected the resortkeeper had seen them; next he had turned in a flash at the girl's cry of warning and had seen her on the porch of the cabin with Dan Farlin, striding down the trail.

The significance of the girl's cry was brought home to him at once. Farlin had seen them or had suspected their meeting, had accused Gladys, who had defied him, and had started out with a threat to shoot him.

Bond raced through the shadows and entered town on the side of the street opposite the Red Arrow. He hurried to the livery and ordered his horse saddled and put in the corral behind the barn, bribing the barn man to secrecy. This bribing might not have been so easy and complete but for the fact that practically no tips were forthcoming from Lester or Farlin, who used horses so little, and, if the barn man suspected anything between Gladys and this young stranger, he—well, the girl was a good tipper, too. Altogether, it was good business for him, for no one had complained to him about Bond, and the latter, too, was to be respected for his horse. The owner of such a horse was no ordinary range rider.

Bond made a quick visit to Porky Snyder's room. He had his gun in his hand, for he was taking no chances. Things were going to blow up soon. Bond felt it, and he had an errand ahead.

The light was turned low in the little gunman's room and Bond put a finger to his lips for caution and was careful that his shadow didn't show against the window shade.

"How you feel, Porky?" he asked in a low voice.

"Better," whispered the gunman. "Lester wants me to get well quick." He grinned. "Says he's got a job for me that'll mean big money." He nodded and winked.

"Probably going to hand you my ticket," said Bond grimly. "Here's five hundred on account. Now Gladys may want to get a message to me, or you may want to reach me yourself. Note the name on this piece of paper but don't speak it aloud."

Porky looked at the name on the slip and his eyes widened.

"Don't speak it," Bond warned softly. "You can reach me through that party. It's all right and you can trust me. I'm sloping out of town for a few days. Things are too hot here because Farlin is sore, Gladys might get in trouble, and there's no telling what Lester might get in his fool head. You're playing along with me?" Bond crumpled the slip of paper and chewed it.

Porky looked at the wad of bills and thrust them under his pillow.

"I'd be a fool not to trail with you," he said. And his tone showed unmistakably that he meant just what he said.

"All right. I'll slope." Bond pressed Porky's hand a moment and slipped silently out of the room. A few minutes later he was riding swiftly into the northeast.

* * * * *

It was Gladys Farlin who first discovered that Bond had left town when she got her horse for an early ride next morning.

"You don't know where he went?" she asked, handing the barn man a folded bill.

"Nope." He grinned. He rather liked the idea of an affair between the good-looking stranger and this attractive girl. Good pay, both of them. "Hinted he'd be back, though," he volunteered.

"I was asking because I'm merely curious," she said, taking up her reins.

Dan Farlin smiled in satisfaction when he heard the news from Lester. He could think of no errand the resortkeeper could have sent him on, and he was pretty sure Bond had made Lester pay plenty in Rocky Point. The logical conclusion was that Bond had seen that he was up against it and had taken the easiest way out. Gladys herself strengthened this conviction when he asked her if she had heard of the fellow's leave-taking. Indeed, he suspected the girl had told him something that had hastened his departure. After all, his daughter was not fool enough to take up with some passing gamester and gunman.

"I'm not interested," she had told him haughtily. "And I don't want to hear any more about it."

"I'm pleased you don't," was his retort. He felt rather ashamed and embarrassed because of his outburst of the night before. He loved this girl too much to injure her feelings willingly. And one thing was sure: they would certainly leave Sunrise as speedily as possible.

* * * * *

Within three days Ed Lawson had returned. He was alone and in an ugly mood. Both Farlin and Lester knew the signals. He had had trouble with his men and had laid down the law to them. Possibly he had had a run-in with Red Cole, and this always put him in a harsh frame of mind. For Cole was the one man in the outfit who came a bit short of being afraid of him. He drank by himself at the upper end of the bar, and it was Dan Farlin who first approached him.

"In for a whirl at the paper beauties?" he asked in a tone loud enough for the listening Lester to hear.

"If I am, I'll make a hard hand in the game," he retorted sharply.

"You never were good for a player's nerves," Farlin commented, raising his brows in significance.

"Give us a drink," Lawson ordered sullenly.

"All of us?" Farlin asked with a wink at Big Tom.

"I'm buyin' in pairs or singles this trip," scowled the outlaw.

Farlin shrugged. "We want to pull this job of ours just as soon as we can," he said in an undertone.

"That'll be within forty-eight hours if you figure you can make it," was the surly answer so that Farlin alone could hear.

"Couldn't be better," said the gambler. Then, in a louder voice for Lester's benefit: "So we will have a little game, eh?"

"Yes, but don't start countin' out the checks till I've had something to eat." The outlaw drained his glass and left.

"What's got into him?" asked Lester anxiously, shortly after.

"Must have had a run-in with some of his men," Farlin replied casually. "Don't worry, he's going to play. I know that breed like a book. He's in town to get whatever's lurking in his system."

Some time later, when Gladys had learned Lawson was back and that her father was playing late that night, she visited Porky Snyder's room under pretense of taking the wounded gunman a glass of homemade jelly. She appeared hesitant and Porky surmised the true nature of her errand. Bond had said she might want to send a message through Porky's hands. Bond was indeed trusting him.

"Sure you ain't got anything for me besides . . . the jelly?" he insinuated subtly.

She looked at him half frightened. "Why should you think that?" she countered.

"Because Jim Bond tipped me off," he said, lowering his voice.

"Tipped you off to what?" she asked in a whisper.

"Said you might want to send him a message through me."
She looked at him for some time.

"Is it all right, Porky?" she asked in a low, even voice.

"You know me, Miss Gladys. An' there must be some good reason for Jim Bond to trust me. Don't you think so?"

She took a long breath, looked at him again, thrust a hand within her jacket, and brought out a letter that she handed to the wounded man in the bed. Then she rose hurriedly.

"I'm trusting you, too, Porky, and, if there's anything I can do for you, let me know. And . . . thank you."

She went out swiftly with a single backward glance.

Porky just had time to slip the envelope, addressed simply to Jim Bond and sealed, under the edge of his pillow when the door flew open and Lester came in, closing the door after him and looking keenly at Porky. He noted, too, the glass of jelly on the stand.

"Findin' out you've got some nice friends, eh, Porky?" Lester's voice held nothing of friendliness, let alone kindness.

Porky's hands slid down beneath the covers. "Sure," he replied brightly. "You an' some others, eh, Tom."

"Jelly!" snorted the resortkeeper with a light sneer. "It'll take something besides jelly to get you well. The doctor told me you wouldn't be out of here for a month, the way you're doin'!"

"Well, the doctor ought to know what he's talkin' about," said Porky in resignation. "Why . . . is that job so pressing?"

"It can't wait a month," said Lester harshly. "Just when I need you bad an' get a good thing for you, you go get shot up turnin' common burglar. That's the way I figure it."

"What is this job?" asked Porky slowly. "Maybe I can fool the doc an' sneak out an' do it without him knowing."

Lester ignored this. "Jelly!" he jeered again. "Did the Farlin girl have anything special to say?" His eyes glowed with suspicion.

"That's a funny thing for *you* to ask," said Porky coldly.

"I want to know where you stand, that's all," snarled Lester. "I heard that Bond or Bovert had sneaked up here to see you. He bores you up at the Farlin place, comes to see you, an' now the girl's sneaking up. I know she didn't just come here to bring you some silly jelly."

"Sometimes you think you know too much," said Porky, and the resortkeeper should have taken warning at the tone of the voice.

"Looks like you was tryin' to double-cross me, if you want to know," said Lester hotly. "Here I've kept you when you couldn't hang out anywhere else for years, an' what do I get?"

"I reckon you get what you're entitled to, Tom."

"Yeah? What's this?" Lester's keen eyes had detected the corner of the envelope Gladys Farlin had left peeping out from under the pillow. He hurled his big bulk forward with surprising agility and grasped it, waving it in triumph.

"Drop it!"

The little gunman's words cut through the room sharply as Lester, his face darkening, read the name on the envelope.

"You insignificant little rat!" he cried, giving Porky a dark look. He tore open the envelope.

"Drop it now!" Porky Snyder's right hand came out from under the covers, grasping his gun in fingers of steel.

Lester's eyes popped, then reddened with rage. "Why you . . ."

Then the bomb to which Lester, among others, had attached the fuse exploded. In his rage, Big Tom forgot himself for an instant and made a move for his weapon.

The crashing report of Porky's gun in the little room fairly rocked it. The envelope and letter fluttered to the floor. Lester's right hand swung over toward his heart and he splintered the chair by the bed as he dropped to the floor.

Porky Snyder leaned over with a groaning effort and recovered the letter and envelope as a stamping of feet was heard on the stairs.

Chapter Twenty-One

The first to burst in the door of Porky Snyder's room was the hotel clerk. He stopped short, aghast, his mouth gaping and his eyes bulging. He looked at the man in the bed foolishly and pointed a shaking finger at the prone figure on the floor with the broken chair scattered grotesquely about.

"What . . . what . . . ?"

"Shut up an' drag it out of here," Porky instructed crisply. "Get it out! He's dead, don't worry about that." He smiled faintly. "An' send for Dan Farlin quick as you can get him," he added sharply.

"But . . . you shot him?" the man gasped out.

"No. I bit him," Porky replied sarcastically. "Get that thing out of here, do you hear?" He half started up in bed in a rage as others crowded into the room, but fell back with a groan. His wound was hurting him badly. He had wrenched it in bending over to get the envelope and message that had fluttered to the floor when Big Tom had leaned forward to his death.

The spectators stared, wide-eyed, stupefied, at the figure on the floor and were awed into silence by the pale, withered man in the bed who still held the big, black gun in his hand against the white counterpane.

Then the clerk ran out the door; there was a scurrying of feet; men running down the stairs, confusion everywhere, and within a minute the news was being cried out by many voices in the street below.

"Porky Snyder has killed Big Tom Lester!"

The shriveled gunman, groaning with the pain in his side, fainted.

When he opened his eyes, Dan Farlin and Ed Lawson were just entering the room. Lawson merely glanced at the body on the floor, but Farlin made a swift examination to be sure that Lester was dead.

"Right through the heart," he muttered as he rose.

"I always had a hunch," Lawson ruminated thoughtfully, "that this would happen someday. Shot him from bed, too." He continued to stare at the killer with an anomalous expression in his cruel eyes as if he were trying to read Porky's thoughts.

"How'd it happen?" Farlin asked briskly to cover up his own confusion and perplexity. He was taken back at the suddenness and completeness of it all. He was one who realized that death is always final.

"He came up here in a huff," Porky explained quietly. "Sore because Miss Gladys brought me a present an' started bawlin' me out. His words had hair on 'em an' I shaved 'em clean. He made a motion for his gun. He oughta known better, that's all."

"Gladys here!" said Farlin, passing a hand over his eyes. "What was the present?"

Porky pointed to the jar of jelly on the stand.

Lawson laughed suddenly, harshly, uproariously.

"Went to the devil over a glass of jam," he managed to get out.

Farlin looked incredulous. For once he didn't know what to do or say. It was all so weird and grotesque, and seemingly unnecessary, that it bordered on the ludicrous. But there was no getting away from the fact that Big Tom Lester lay at his feet dead.

"You better go over an' take charge of the place," Porky advised. "You're the one to do it. An' that's why I sent for you."

At this point the doctor came into the room.

"Come on, Dan," said Lawson. "Porky's got that much sense anyway."

Porky wasn't interested in what the doctor had to say, or conscious, apparently, of the excitement that went on about him as they carried out Lester's body. The wound in his side was causing him great pain. He hesitated to tell the doctor about it because he didn't want to be uncovered for an examination. He wanted first to read the contents of the message Gladys Farlin had entrusted to him to be sent to its destination and then destroy it. After what had happened, he knew Sheriff Mills would come to Sunrise as fast as possible. And Bond had instructed him to forward any message to him to the sheriff through the night man at the livery.

When he was finally left temporarily alone, he managed to read the lines Gladys had penciled and found the communication was merely concerned with the fact that Lawson had returned to town and that her father was acting queerly.

"No need to send that for the sheriff will be here quick enough," muttered Porky. "An' if he knows where Bond is, why Bond will know as soon as he does. Chances are they'll both be here by daybreak."

He tore up the envelope, which was inscribed merely to Bond, since the latter had told him and no one else where to send it, and then tore up the message. How to dispose of them was the next problem and that was easily solved. Porky had tobacco, papers, and matches. He lighted a match and ignited the paper, watched it burn on the ashtray on the stand at the head of his bed. Then he blew the ashes from the tray and lay back, groaning in pain, but content. He felt no remorse whatsoever for having done for Lester. Lawson had said he had always had a hunch this thing would come to pass someday, and Porky now was cognizant of the fact that he had always had the same hunch. He had done Lester's dirty work and had been treated like a rat in return. It was his own fault, perhaps, but was it all his fault? He thought not and dismissed the matter from his mind. But why had Porky gone in with Bond? For money? He decided to the contrary. Because he hated Lawson for refusing to take him into his band of outlaws? No, again. Dan Farlin had always treated him squarely and he always had admired the splendid man of chance. He had always secretly admired Gladys. Her songs had brought the only bits of joy that had brightened his life. He had thrown in with Bond because he hadn't wanted Dan Farlin to go all wrong. Satisfied with this he dropped off into troubled sleep.

* * * * *

The Red Arrow was in an uproar. Gaming devices and tables were deserted and the throng was crowding the bar and gathering in excited groups, talking, gesticulating, shouting, swearing, wondering what was to happen next, stunned by the sudden passing of the big boss and speculating as to the outcome. After all, to most of these men, and hundreds of others, the Red Arrow was Sunrise. The bartenders were attending to their duties with six-shooters on either side of the cash boxes. The safe was locked— Farlin had seen to that. For the time being the notorious resort was without a head. But not for long.

Dan Farlin came in, cool, his face a bit more stern than usual. He was followed by Ed Lawson, who looked alertly about with a scowl. The outlaw took his place at the lower end of the bar, but Farlin went around behind it to a central position and held up a hand. The crowd was instantly silenced, straining its ears and eyes.

"Boys, Big Tom is dead," Farlin announced in a clear voice that carried distinctly to every ear. "Porky Snyder shot him a short while ago up at the hotel. You all know Porky was hurt and in bed with the doc looking after him. Tonight he was delirious when Big Tom went up to see him. Porky never was without his gun, you know that. He had it in bed with him. We don't know how it happened, but all we can make out is that Porky shot and killed Big Tom without knowing what he was doing. Maybe he didn't know it was Big Tom he was shooting. But it's done, and . . ." He paused, looking grimly at the sea of faces before him. "Business will go on as usual, for the present. I'm taking charge of the place."

He nodded convincingly to the crowd, looked sharply at the bartenders who nodded back.

"That's all," Farlin concluded. "But don't start anything!"

One long look at the gambler's stern features, another at the fearsome frown of Lawson, standing ready to back up the speaker, and the crowd knew the Red Arrow had a new boss.

A short cheer went up as Farlin and Lawson disappeared into the little office that had been Lester's. Then the scores of voices buzzed again, the bartenders grew active, the wheels whirred, dice rattled, dealers called for players at the poker tables, the piano sounded, and a sweet voice floated out over the throng. Gladys Farlin back!

The cheering this time was lusty and long.

When Gladys returned to her dressing room, she met her father, his face a veritable thundercloud.

"What are you doing here?" he demanded hoarsely.

"I'm helping to calm the crowd," she replied in a cool voice. "I knew you would do this the minute I heard what had happened. I want to help you keep out of danger. Those men are liable to stampede the place."

Dan Farlin struggled with his voice. "I'll calm the crowd," he declared huskily. "And if I'm not enough, Ed Lawson and others are here to help me. This is a bad time for you to be out there singing, sweetie. Please, *please*"—he was genuinely pleading— "go back home. Your being here bothers me and if I was to lose my nerve . . ." He let her draw her own inference.

Gladys's cheeks paled. "Is it as bad as that, Daddy?" she suddenly asked in a whisper.

"It's liable to be as bad as that . . . and maybe worse," was the grim answer. "I've got to keep things even here. I've started and I'm going through. You didn't know it, but I was practically a . . . a silent partner in this place. Now, will you go?"

"If you promise me there's no danger . . ." She stopped, helpless.

"There's no danger," said Dan Farlin in a strong voice.

"Then I'll go," she said, kissing him impulsively and turning away.

Farlin went back to the private office.

Lawson was sitting at Lester's desk when he entered. He looked at Lawson twice because he didn't like the expression in the outlaw's eyes. He saw, too, that Lawson had been rummaging in the drawers of Lester's desk. He didn't like this, either, and rolled a cigarette to regain his composure. He knew what was in the outlaw's mind as well as if the latter had shouted it to him when he entered.

"She goin' home?" asked Lawson, exhaling cigar smoke.

"Gladys, you mean?" Farlin's brows tilted at the other's easy familiarity. "Yes, she's leaving. This is no time for her here."

Lawson leaned forward. "But it's a great time for us, Dan," he said in a significant tone with a side glance at the safe.

"I know what you mean"—Farlin nodded—"but it isn't in the picture. It would be like suicide."

"Yeah?" sneered the outlaw. "You goin' to leave this place untapped? Why, it's just the same as if it fell into our lap. Lester left plenty in that safe, an' there's money at the bar an' on the tables."

"Sure," Farlin agreed. "But there isn't as much as you think. Lester's been afraid right along that you'd raid this place and he has his planted. What's here is working capital. I've seen him have to go out for more, and more than once. Where he's got it, I don't know. You can have it if you can find it, but you can lay your last white marker that he didn't have what he's got outside the banks hidden where anybody is going to find it easily."

"There's enough around here to bother with," said Lawson confidently.

Farlin turned on him angrily. "Are you a fool?" he demanded. "You've got to blow that safe to get what's in it and you've got to work the rest in person. The marks and wagging tongues would be left. And what we'd get here wouldn't be a two-cent stamp to what the haul will be in the Point."

Lawson's eyes had narrowed.

"You needn't get so huffy about it. I hate to pass it up, that's all. Somebody's goin' to get it, that's a cinch." He was growing angry.

Farlin sat down close to him. "Let 'em get it," he said. "But they won't get it while I'm here and you're not going to be here, for it's your play to beat it. Don't you know that Mills will be here as quick as he hears about this? Don't you suppose the word's on the way to him right now? Say, you don't know the smug busybodies that live here the year around like I do. The sheriff will be here *pronto*. If the place were gutted, he'd blame you first off. What's to stop me from telling him that you beat it because you were afraid he'd think you had something to do with the business? Don't you think I know him and know how to talk to him? You don't want any hand in this in any way, shape, or manner."

Lawson was considering this thoughtfully.

"May be something in what you've got to say," he conceded.

"And I'm not through talking," said Farlin. "This is the biggest kind of a break of luck for us, but not in the way you think. Listen. This'll bring Mills here, probably with a couple of his bright-eyed deputies. All right. He'll be out of Rocky Point, won't he? There'll be no sheriff at the Point. And while he's out of the Point, we'll take the bank down there. Why, man, it's made to order."

Lawson's eyes took on a gleam.

"By thunder, you're right!" he ejaculated. "You've got the brains, Dan. That's why I let you in on the play at the Point. Lester's killin' was the first stroke of luck, an' now, with you here to protect the play an' steer Mills off the track, well . . . it's the second stroke of luck. We're goin' to team up well." He thought a minute. "How you goin' to dodge out of here to get to the Point an' when?" he asked with a trace of suspicion in his voice.

You leave that to me," was Farlin's answer. "When can you have your outfit over at Crazy?"

"Tomorrow night, of course," replied Lawson quickly.

"All right, I'll be in Rocky Point by ten o'clock tomorrow night," said Farlin. "I know the lay of the land and every step to make . . . just when and how to make it. I'll do the work here and you can do the work over there. But don't try to cross me, Ed. I'm in this thing and I'm going through with it. But if you try to cross me . . . even if you kill me . . . I've provided for that, Ed, and don't kid yourself into thinking I haven't."

"Cut out the crossin' talk." Lawson scowled. He didn't like what Farlin had said. The man was clever. Maybe he was too clever. He wasn't particularly afraid of the man's snaky draw and sure shooting. But he had to confess that he was afraid of his brain. "What's my next move, then?" he asked in a surly tone.

"Go get your men and get over there," Farlin snapped out. "And don't let anybody know you're leaving town."

"Jake with me," said the outlaw, rising. "We'll take a snort at the bar an' I'll call out that I'll be back later."

Neither of them would have been as much at ease if they had known that Red Cole and Jim Bond were meeting that very minute at the edge of town.

Chapter Twenty-Two

It was purely by chance that Lawson's chief lieutenant, Red Cole, and Jim Bond met just at the edge of the trees outside the limit of the town, behind the livery. They came upon each other suddenly, so suddenly, in fact, that each whipped out his gun. Bond had come from the east, and Cole had come from the west. There was a curve here and each was trying to get to the livery without being seen in the street. As they rounded the curve, they nearly clashed. But they recognized each other quickly in the moonlight.

"'Lo, Cole," drawled Bond, bringing his horse to a standstill. "You're in a day or two early, aren't you?"

"Reckon I came in for the same reason you did," Cole retorted. "I didn't think Porky had it in him."

"Neither did I," Bond answered quickly. He didn't know what the other was talking about, but from the nature of Cole's remark he instantly surmised that Porky Snyder had done something, and, by the other's tone, that something had been keen work. "How bad is it?" he asked, taking the chance that his query might bring information.

"Lester's dead," said Cole bluntly. "So the man I got the news from said, an' you know Porky was a tolerably fair shot. Never thought he'd have spunk enough to do it, although Big Tom's had it comin' to him for a long time. I half expected it."

"So did I," said Bond, his mind working fast. "How'd it happen?"

173

"Dunno," Cole confessed. "Goin' to make any difference with your game?" He tried to put the question offhandedly.

"Might help it," said Bond mysteriously. "But we better not stay here talking. Somebody might hear or see us. Slide along in and I'll follow. I'll see you later."

"Good idea," Cole agreed. "So long." He rode into the trees.

Bond didn't go to the barn. Instead, he tied his horse in the trees at the edge of town near where the trail led east from the main street. He hadn't received Gladys Farlin's letter, or message, of course, but he knew one thing—what had evidently happened would most certainly speed the plans of Farlin and Lawson, unless . . . There was the rub. If Lester really were dead, Farlin might take over the resort. And this was one thing Bond didn't want him to do. He didn't want him to do anything that might interfere with Bond's desire to win Gladys. He decided that, if Lester were dead, Farlin certainly wouldn't be home. Would Gladys be home? Would it be safe to try to see her? He thought a long time and decided it was worth the chance.

* * * * *

When Red Cole reached the livery, he lost no time in learning what he could about the shooting of Lester by Porky Snyder. As he listened to the excited barn man, he began to turn on his toes with a show of nervousness. His eyes narrowed and his teeth closed over his upper lip.

"Sounds fishy to me," he commented. "Something's behind it."

"That's what everybody else thinks," said the barn man.

"Shut up!" exclaimed Cole as he passed the man some money. "An' don't tell anybody you was talkin' to me. Lawson's still in town, eh?"

"Sure," was the answer. "But his hoss is ready."

Cole stopped short on his way to the front entrance. Lester dead and Lawson leaving so soon? Cole's eyes narrowed to slits. "Ready to beat it, eh?" he said sharply.

"Looks that way," was the noncommittal answer.

"Get out of sight," Cole ordered quickly. Then he himself stepped out of the light of the lantern hanging over the wide door. He was cursing softly.

Ed Lawson was walking briskly toward the barn from the hotel. He was carrying a saddlebag and Cole couldn't remember if the chief had taken a saddlebag to town from the camp a few miles out or not. In any event, it didn't look too good, considering the conclusion Cole had reached.

As Lawson entered the barn, Cole stepped out in full view. "Hello, chief," he greeted amiably.

Lawson halted and glared. "What're you doin' in town this soon?" he demanded. "Or at all?" he added angrily.

"I had no orders before tomorrow," said Cole coolly, "and I came in for a snort or two before the big doings. I didn't reckon you'd kick."

"You're meanin' you sneaked in, thinking I wouldn't be here," said Lawson in a nasty tone accompanied by a hard look. He shifted the saddlebag from his right hand to his left and the move wasn't lost on Cole.

"I didn't care whether you were here or not," Cole shot back. "What's this I hear about Porky killin' Lester?"

"It's just what you heard," Lawson snapped. "What of it?" It was the second time within twenty-four hours that a clash with his henchman had appeared imminent.

Cole stepped closer. "Porky didn't kill Big Tom without some good reason," he said in a low voice. "An' he had a good chance to do it with him in bed an' Lester unsuspecting, eh?"

Lawson dropped the bag. "What're you gettin' at?" he asked.

"What you got in the bag?" Cole demanded sternly.

Lawson gasped. Then his jaw came up and he leaned forward. "So that's what you've got in that thick, fool head of yours!"

"Never mind what I've got in my head. What have you got in the bag." Cole was in deadly earnest and his voice attested to it.

Lawson's face purpled. "What do you think?" he snarled.

"Money," said Cole steadily. "Money from the Red Arrow!"

Lawson, boiling with rage, gritted his teeth. "You think it was a job, eh?"

"I'm not as big a fool as you think," replied Cole. "You've asked for information, now you'll get it. You paid Porky off to do for Lester so you could clean out the safe. Porky takes the blame for the killin' . . . at a price. You figured to clean up here on the side an' leave me out in the cold, watching the soldiers. For all I know this Rocky Point raid is a bluff. If it isn't, you'll split with me on this, old scout." His face was livid at the thought of being double-crossed and not for an instant did he take his eyes from Lawson.

The outlaw leader laughed in his face. "You've got more imagination than you've got brains, Red. If I'd wanted to take Lester's place, I'd have taken it long ago an' you know it."

"I don't know anything about what you'd have done long ago," was the answer. "I only care what's been done tonight. If I hadn't happened along . . ."

"If you hadn't happened along, you'd be better off," hissed Lawson. "At that, I'll give you a chance to go along with me."

"An' get a slug in the back?" jeered Cole. "Show me!"

"Show you what?" asked Lawson in a dangerous, silky voice.

"Open the bag!" Cole commanded.

"That does it," said Lawson through his teeth. "You don't have to take it in the back. You can take it standing up."

"Try it!" Cole's words rang through the barn.

With the swiftness of light the men's tight hands moved and the guns blazed almost as one in the yellow gleam of the lantern. Cole stood stockstill after the first two shots, and then Lawson's weapon spit its death flash of fire the second time. Still Cole stood, his eyes glassy in the lantern light. Suddenly he crumpled in a queer heap on the floor of the barn.

Lawson grabbed his saddlebag and darted into the barn office where the night man stood, trembling.

"You heard what he said!" cried the outlaw, grasping the man's arm. "He brought it on himself. There's been no robbery. This bag has my things in it. It was a fair gun play, understand? Fair gun play! Get my horse out quick, an' then get word to Dan Farlin at the Red Arrow that I've bumped off Cole. Move!"

The man moved, and by the time the shots had brought cautious persons to the scene, he was on his way with the message for Farlin.

Farlin took the news calmly enough. He sensed instantly that the shooting of Cole provided an excellent excuse for Lawson's hurried departure from town. Moreover, Cole's demise removed one disturbing factor from the prospective aftermath of the projected raid at Rocky Point. And his services were not essential in the bank undertaking. He spoke swiftly and earnestly to the barn man.

"Remember exactly what Lawson told you," he said. "You heard them talking, as you say. And it was a fair gun play. The sheriff will question you and you simply tell him the truth. You can see for yourself that there's been no robbery here, and I'll give you my word, which you know is good, that there isn't going to be any. So that's all. And here's a ten-dollar bill to quiet your nerves."

* * * * *

Jim Bond rapped boldly upon the front door of the Farlin cabin. It was Gladys herself who responded.

She caught her breath and stepped back, motioning for him to enter.

"However did you get my message so soon?" she asked as she closed the door.

"I didn't receive any message," he replied in surprise. "I just happened along. Did you give a message for me to Porky?"

"Just before the . . . the shooting," she answered. "Oh, Jim Bond, it's . . . it's terrible!" There was a catch in her voice.

"Now tell me quickly what has happened, Gladys," he said earnestly. "This may make things different and I can't stay here long, as you know. Tell me what you know, girlie."

Gladys explained her visit to Porky Snyder, detailing the incident of entrusting the message to his care.

"It was just to tell you that Lawson was back and that Father was acting, well . . . acting stranger than I ever saw him act before," she said, trembling. "And I was so worried . . . I thought you ought to know Lawson was here."

"That's right." He nodded. "And Lester went up to see Porky right after you left. He must have, because the shooting took place so soon. Now I understand it. Lester got hold of that note in some way and Porky shot him. It's as plain as daylight. Well, Lester is no great loss and I'll protect Porky." He thought a few moments. "And your dad's in charge down at the place? Yes? And Lawson's still here? Well, unless my thinking cap's got a hole in it, Lawson will be beating it *pronto*. He will . . ."

Bond's speech stopped suddenly and they stood staring at each other in startled apprehension. For three shots had broken sharply on the night air.

Gladys stifled a scream and started for the door, but Bond caught her and held her.

"Don't get excited," he said. "You can't go out, and . . ."

"It's Daddy!" cried the girl. "Lawson has shot him! I *know* that Lawson has shot him to rob the place."

"Don't you ever think it," he said convincingly in her ear. "I happen to know that, if there is one thing Lawson doesn't want to do, it's shoot your father. I'll tell you something else. Now be quiet and don't start going to pieces. Red Cole just rode into town. I'd bet every dollar I've got and my horse, saddle, and gun that he and Lawson have come together. Now you stay here and I'll go down and sneak around a bit and find out. Then I'll come back. I won't be long. Please be yourself, Gladys . . . for me."

The girl recovered almost instantly and looked up at him.

"Go ahead, Jim, only . . . be sure to come back. I trust you."

Bond kissed her, and smiled. "Gladys, I'd bet my life on my hunch that everything's coming out all right. Dog-gone, I'm beginning to feel downright happy."

A few moments later he hurried away, and Gladys sank upon a divan. Her head was swimming. Jim Bond—Bovert—gunman and killer! She laughed foolishly. Lester dead! And now . . . She went into her bedroom and sat by the window. There was no light in the room and she could see the path to town where yellow gleams of lamplight glowed like paper lanterns among the trees and dark shadows of dingy buildings. She was watching, waiting until *her man* came back.

* * * * *

Jim Bond circled through the trees until he reached the rear of the livery. He saw the crowd in front and sensed at once that here was where the shooting had taken place. By the time he reached the place, Lawson had ridden away and the night man was returning after having delivered his message to Dan Farlin. The barn man was entering the barn from the rear to avoid the crowd. Bond stopped him and speedily learned what had taken place.

"You're sure Lawson has gone?" Bond said thoughtfully.

"He left right after," the man replied.

"All right," said Bond. "Saddle Gladys Farlin's horse and get it out here. She wants it, understand, as quick as she can get it and I'm going to take it to her. And all this is under your hat." There was an exchange of gold.

The request didn't seem unreasonable to the barn man. Hadn't Gladys herself been interested in this stranger? He thrilled with an inspiring thought. An elopement! He was past asking the reason why for anything. The town was blowing up and he knew it. He prepared immediately to follow instructions.

Bond's attempt to see Porky Snyder proved futile. The sick man was worse. He was in a raving delirium and the doctor was with him. Bond went back to the livery and in a short time he had Gladys's horse tethered beside his own near the trail that led out of town eastward.

Gladys saw him coming and was at the door, opening it, before he could rap. One look at his face and she gave a little cry of joy, for she knew her father was safe.

"Lawson shot Cole and sloped," said Bond crisply. "Now you and I have something to do. Get your riding clothes on as quick as you can, make up a little pack of things you may absolutely need, and hurry . . . above all things, Gladys, do not ask questions, for they take time. The main thing is to hurry. We're leaving town."

"But, Jim . . ."

"Do as I say, Gladys," he commanded sternly. "We're going to Rocky Point. By tomorrow night your father and Lawson will be there. Lawson's gone for his gang. I know what I'm talking about. You've got to play the game with me or we'll lose. Now, do you believe me?"

Gladys believed him. Figuratively she threw everything to the wide winds and hurried to do as he had directed. She told the housekeeper she was going with Bond, as he suggested. The Negro woman danced about in excitement and hugged and kissed her as she left.

In the short space of half an hour they were riding swiftly across the plain of flowing shadows toward the jagged outline of Crazy Butte that stood out against the stars.

Chapter Twenty-Three

Dan Farlin had many friends in Sunrise. Now that Cole was dead and Lawson, as report had it, had fled as the result, he sent for several of his closest friends to stand by in the Red Arrow in event that any of the hard characters frequenting the place should attempt to raid it. Employees had definite instructions to shoot and shoot straight at the start of trouble. Meanwhile he had a visitor in the person of Smith, proprietor of the general store, and, as such, the leading merchant.

"I sent word to Mills the moment I heard what had taken place," said Smith gravely. "It was my duty as . . . well, you know I'm supposed to be special deputy here and the sheriff ordered me to get word to him in case anything like the killing of Lester occurred. He didn't care so much about shootings among the crowd that comes to town . . . well, you know." He wiped his forehead.

"Yes, I know," said Farlin. "I'm glad you sent word. I'm just looking after this place till the sheriff gets here. I thought it was up to me, seeing that I'd sort of worked with Lester so long. That business between Lawson and Cole was just an outlaw shooting and won't do the town any harm."

"That's right," Smith nodded. "Maybe this is all going to be good for the town, although I haven't got any ranch business to speak of, and of course I don't want to do anything that would . . . hurt things."

Farlin remembered again what John Duggan, the banker, had said about the prospective influx of homesteaders.

"You haven't hurt things any," he assured the merchant. "Just let matters ride and things will adjust themselves."

"I'm hoping you will take over this place, Farlin," said Smith as he turned' to go. "My girl and yours are good friends, for one thing, and I believe you'd run it on better lines, for another thing. Of course it's none of my business." He paused before Farlin's cold look. "If you want me for anything, send word," he said, and left.

Farlin went into the private office after the merchant had gone out and sat down at Lester's desk, leaving the door open. In the big room of the resort, business was going on much as usual, although there was an undercurrent of excitement, augmented by the killing of Cole.

The astute gambler was considering the possibility of taking over the Red Arrow. Why not? Even if the end of Sunrise as a wide-open, lawless town was in sight—provided Duggan knew what he was talking about, and there was every reason to believe he did—there always would be good business for a place such as this. And a legitimate business, at that. Still, Farlin couldn't seize it outright. Lester had heirs; he had often spoken in a guarded way of a sister, for one thing. Farlin would have to buy the place. In order to buy the place he would have to sacrifice the big ranch in Texas and accept a substantial loss. Moreover, he had Gladys's ideas in the matter to consider. Furthermore, he had Ed Lawson to reckon with. He had gone into the Rocky Point raid proposition with Lawson and had given his word. If he broke it, it could mean but one thing—one thing *only*. He would have to shoot it out with the outlaw whose very name inspired terror when there was talk of gun play. How easily he had disposed of the formidable Cole. Farlin suddenly felt old. He was fearless, but down in the bottom of his heart he knew he was no match for Lawson when it came to guns. Again he had to think of Gladys. No, he had to go through with the raid. He rolled a cigarette with steady fingers and went out for a small drink.

At dawn Farlin considered going up to the cabin. He decided that Gladys would not be up before 7:00, when the bartenders changed shift, and he would have to assume charge of the night's takings. So he waited, made up the cash, and put matters in order for the day. The crowd had thinned to less than a score. He placed the head bartender in charge and thrust the bag of money in his pocket. He had closed the outer door of the safe and twirled the combination as soon as he had learned of Lester's death. Naturally he did not know the combination, nor did any of the men who worked in the place. One thing was certain. He would relinquish his supervision of the resort upon the arrival of Sheriff Mills, who, he suspected, would close it temporarily at least.

The sun was shining brightly, striking a brilliant green from the leaves of the graceful cottonwoods and poplars. The air was soft with the subtle tang of spring. Birds were singing and the world seemed a thing of beauty. Sunrise! Never was a town better named, thought Farlin as he walked up the trail to the white cabin, with its apron of green lawn, its lilacs and colorful flower beds. He was alive, he was healthy, he had a beautiful daughter who he loved and who loved him—he was lucky. Just one last play.

Gladys didn't answer when he rapped gently on her door. He called softly. Surely she hadn't resented his request that she go home the night before. He looked around as the housekeeper came into the living room from the kitchen. For several moments he looked at her keenly, then he strode toward her swiftly.

"Has Gladys gone riding?" he asked. "Is she up?"

"Why, Mister Farlin, boss, she went last night," was the answer.

A number of expressions came into Dan Farlin's face and fled, leaving it stern and white. He grasped the Negro woman by an arm.

"Last night? What do you mean?" he thundered.

"She went away with Mister Bond," replied the housekeeper in a frightened voice. "Didn't you know?"

Farlin flung her aside and stood as if stunned. "Why . . . why didn't you tell me . . . send word . . . why . . . ?" His words broke off in a mumble and the look in his eyes became hard, steel-blue. "Did she say where she . . . they . . . were going?" he asked dully.

But the woman was too frightened to talk. She shook her head, turned, and fled to her own room off the kitchen.

Farlin walked swiftly to Gladys's bedroom, threw open the door, and looked in. Everything was in confusion. In a moment he ascertained that Gladys's favorite riding habit and boots were gone. He went into his own bedroom, and put the money he carried in the wall safe behind the picture. Then he left the cabin.

If anyone who knew Dan Farlin well could have seen his face as he walked swiftly down the trail to town, they would have stopped short, struck with wonder and concern. His features were set and cold, his eyes hard as flint, his lips pressed so tightly together that they formed a white line like a scar. He gripped his palms. Something had gone out of his heart, and something terrible had entered it.

He walked straight to the livery. There he looked for Gladys's horse and found it gone. He confronted the night man, who still was there, although off duty.

"How long since Gladys got her horse?" he asked icily.

"Why . . . she didn't get it," replied the man, startled by the gambler's look and manner and tone.

The deadly, snub-nosed Derringer dropped like magic into Farlin's right hand. He shoved its nose against the man's stomach. "One more lie and I'm going to let you have it for keeps," he said.

"I'm tellin' the truth, so help me!" shrieked the other in fearful dread of those burning eyes. "That fellow Bond got it . . . after the shootings. Said she sent him for it. So help me that's the truth. I didn't mean no harm, I . . ."

But Farlin had swung on his heel. He almost had expected the answer and he knew the man had spoken the truth. He proceeded to the hotel, and went up to Porky's room.

The little gunman, his face drawn and his eyes sunken from the effects of the fever, his wound throbbing with a steady excruciating pain, stared dully at him from the depth of his pillow.

But the sight had no effect upon Dan Farlin. "Can you hear me, Porky?" he asked hoarsely.

The sick man's lips formed the word: "Yes."

Farlin leaned over him. The Derringer still was in his hand. "Porky, you're no better than Lester was. The town didn't lose much in him and it wouldn't lose much in you . . . or me, for that matter. Gladys came down here last night and after that you gave Lester his. Now Gladys is gone. *Gone* . . . understand? She's gone with that rotter of a Bovert who calls himself Bond. Do you hear? There was an inside to this killing up here, Porky, and I want it. Gladys didn't come down here just to give a scum like you a glass of jelly. You know something and that something has to do with Gladys's running away with that rat. Tell me the inside, Porky . . . tell me what you know, or just as sure as I know how to pull this trigger, I'll blow you to Kingdom Come!"

A thin smile came to Porky's lips and a faint flush stained his withered cheeks. He spoke with a great effort. "It looks . . . like . . . I'd have . . . to go anyway, Dan. Pull!"

The Derringer came up on a level with Porky's fluttering heart and then Dan Farlin flung himself from the bed. He stood in the center of the room, trembling. What good would it do? What good would anything do? What . . . ?

He went to the window and flung up the shade to let the glad world in. For moments—a minute—minutes he stood there. Then he abruptly left the room. He went back to the Red Arrow and took a drink. They looked at him strangely there. He went into the little office and sat down to wait. After a time he sent out for coffee and breakfast. He drank no more.

Sheriff Mills came shortly before noon.

Sitting in the office, an unlighted cigar between his teeth, never taking his eyes from the speaker's face, the official listened to Dan Farlin's crisp, succinct explanation of what had taken place the night before.

"And that's the story," the gambler finished. "It's all I know, all I've got to say. I've stayed here and kept an eye on things. Nothing has been taken. I'll bring last night's receipts down from the cabin and then I'm turning the place over to you to do with as you confounded please. The rest of your information you can get from Porky, from the barn . . . from anywhere you want, but you've got my end of it."

With this Farlin shot him a look that came near being a look of hatred and undying malice.

The sheriff removed his cigar. "I believe what you say, of course," he said slowly. "But what's the matter with you, Dan? This thing hasn't hit you this hard, has it? It had to come, one way or another. You've got sense enough to see that. And it may be that it spells the end of Sunrise as a bad town. Maybe you see that, too. But you shouldn't take it so much to heart."

Farlin's laugh was so strange that men out in front looked at each other as they heard its echo.

"Listen, you," said Farlin bitterly. "Do you know what's happened?"

"Why, you've just told me, Dan," said the sheriff quietly.

Farlin laughed again. "I haven't told you anything," he sneered. "Nothing! Do you think these killings amount to anything to me? I'd just as soon ride out of this town through a river of blood! Do you think this place was my life? Do you think that, you simple cow sheriff? You ass! Telling us to protect Bovert . . . to leave him alone, which was the same thing. And now what? Because he was good-looking, and had a smooth tongue in his head, and made a few brave plays he's . . . Gladys has run away with him!"

Farlin fairly shouted the words in accusation at the sheriff. Mills looked at him coldly. "How do you know?" he asked.

"Find her!" Farlin fairly hissed. "Go out and find her! Go up to the cabin, comb the town. Ask questions. Find him! And you sit there and talk to me. I played square with you. If you wanted this devil, why didn't you take him? You didn't have the nerve! You weren't sure, you hemmed and hawed, you sat around with your feet on your desk and a cigar in your mouth, waiting for George to do it! Now he's made a fool out of all of us, and Gladys, too. But there's one thing he can't do." Farlin nodded grimly. "He can't outrun a bullet!"

"That'll do," said Mills sternly. "Get out somewhere and try to come to. Then I'll talk to you. Just now I've got other things to do."

* * * * *

Within the hour Dan Farlin was riding east on the trail to Crazy Butte and Rocky Point. So Lawson thought he was bad, eh? The gambler laughed and spurred his horse. No soreness in the saddle now. Just a burning rage that suffused his whole being. He would stage the raid and it was Lawson who would have to look after himself instead of secretly planning to cross another.

And as Farlin rode, so Lawson and his band rode—almost at the butte.

Chapter Twenty-Four

Dawn bloomed like an exquisite white rose in the east when Jim Bond and Gladys Farlin came in sight of Rocky Point. Bond drew rein and smiled at the girl who had ridden with him from Sunrise without asking a question. They had talked a little, but all Bond had told her was that Lawson had intrigued her father into going in with him on a job, and that the job was scheduled for this coming night.

"You will have to go to the hotel, Gladys," he told her, "and I'll have to keep out of sight. Maybe we both better keep out of sight. This is planned as a last job by Lawson, and your dad is figuring the same way. If it goes through, they'll make a clean-up."

"Do you want to tell me what it is, Jim?" she asked.

"I will have to tell you now," he replied gravely. "I could have told you back in Sunrise, but I was afraid you might let something slip. You know . . . without intending to do so. You must promise even now to keep what I tell you a secret. Do you promise?"

"Of course," Gladys answered readily. "I'm trusting you. Do you think I would have ridden here with you if I hadn't decided to trust you?"

"You more than trust me, Gladys," he said softly. "Whether you know it or not, you love me." He saw her cheeks flush with the same delicate glow of pink that was staining the eastern sky. "But we won't talk of that now," he said hastily. "Lawson and your father plan to raid the Rocky Point bank tonight."

"Oh!" The girl's right hand flew to her breast.

"Lawson didn't dare to come to the Point to get the lay of the land and plan the raid. So he got your dad to do that. He admires your father's brain and let him in on it because it was a job that required brains . . . more gray matter than Lawson has. If they are left alone, I believe they can turn the trick and loot the bank. It would mean a lot of money to your dad, Gladys, and, if you say hands off, it's all right with me."

She looked at him quickly and shook her head. "You're just testing me, Jim Bond," she said with a smile. "You know I wouldn't have it that way even if I was certain Father never would be found out."

"That's the way I figured it." He nodded, his eyes shining with approval. "I'm going to make the raid fail, but I'm not telling the banker or anyone else here a thing about it. I'm going to stop it myself. Maybe, when your dad finds you're gone, he won't go through with it. But there's always Lawson to be reckoned with. If your dad didn't go through with it, he would have to shoot it out with Lawson, and . . . well, Lawson is the devil himself with a gun."

Gladys made no comment. She knew this was only too true. Since her father had joined Lawson in this venture, he had to go through with it. Otherwise, Lawson would consider he had been double-crossed and that could mean but one thing—a gun play.

"Are you . . . sure of . . . all this?" she faltered.

"If I wasn't," Bond began—then he paused and looked at the girl closely. "Porky told me," he said. "Lester told him to trail your dad because Lester was afraid your dad was figuring to blow. Porky overheard a conversation between Lawson and your dad when Lawson made his proposition. You can't blame your dad for taking him up on it. Gladys, I know Dan Farlin well enough to know that he wants to quit the . . . the big game. And he wants to leave you fixed right when he quits. You know what I mean. You can't blame him. I don't."

There was a mist in Gladys's eyes and her lips trembled.

"Your dad isn't Lawson's kind," Bond went on quickly. "And if they went through with this business, Lawson would try to cross him, sure as shooting, and maybe kill him. He was glad of the chance to plug Cole and don't you forget it. I spied on their camp and heard 'em planning this raid and heard Lawson have words with Cole. So you can see just what kind of a chance your dad is taking. But you needn't worry. Now, listen, Gladys. You'll have to go into town alone. You've been there before, haven't you?"

"Yes." The girl nodded.

"All right. You'll have to take a room in the hotel, and maybe you'd better stay there, Gladys. If your father comes in ahead of Lawson and his crowd, he'll maybe find out you're there. It doesn't make any difference. It might be better. I'm stopping this raid alone, Gladys, without asking help from anyone. And . . . regardless of what you may think, or find out later . . . I'm not the law, girlie. Do not forget that. I'm not the law!"

She stared in fascination at the grim look on his face and the cold hard look in his eyes. But he wasn't looking at her.

"You're taking a chance yourself, are you not, Jim?" she asked in a low voice.

"For you," he answered quickly. "But let that out. You go into town and get your room. Maybe you better stay there. But please don't say anything to anybody. Do you promise?"

She thought for a time. "All right, Jim Bond, I'll take a chance on you. I won't say a word to a soul."

"That's the girlie!" he exclaimed. "Edge that horse over here so I can give you a kiss and then go on in. The rest of it is up to me."

But Gladys wondered just the same as she rode into Rocky Point. Why had Bond wanted her to leave Sunrise? When her father discovered she was gone, he might give up the bank robbery plan and start looking for her. Then the trouble would come with Lawson just the same. Lawson's killing of Cole showed he was determined and desperate. But Bond had told her in a tone she recognized as conveying the truth that he was not the law. He had said he was going to prevent the bank robbery alone. Therefore, he must know the way the raid was to be staged and what to do. This thought worried the girl but a few moments. She put spurs to her horse and rode on into the Point with her cheeks flushed, her eyes dancing, her blood tingling in her veins. She was putting her trust in an outlaw. It seemed a fitting climax to her wild, prairie career.

George Reed, handsome, genial proprietor of the hotel, was delighted to see her and readily agreed to keep her presence secret without asking any questions. She learned later that Sheriff Mills and his deputies had left town for Sunrise. The coast, then, was clear for the bank raid. But was the coast clear for Jim Bond? She worried, and thrilled, and wondered all day in her room, and after supper took up a position at her window where she could see down the main street.

* * * * *

Never in his life had Bond been so careful of his movements as he was this day. He gained a post of vantage in the wild wastes about Crazy Butte literally by inches. His caution and alertness were so acute that the snapping of a twig brought his gun leaping into his hand. He knew there was a possibility that the disappearance of Gladys might cause Farlin to give up the bank project. In which event, Bond would have only Lawson to deal with. He was going to have to deal with him in any event, consequently it was policy to keep an eye on the outlaw leader rather than on Farlin.

So it was that Bond saw Lawson gather his band in the breaks south of the butte after leaving Gladys. He had heard the excited conversation just outside the outlaws' camp near Sunrise between Cole and Lawson that had ended in harsh words.

"There'll be just three of us to do the real job," Lawson had said. "You an' me an' . . . another. We'll keep the gang back to stop a posse if necessary an' go into town by ourselves."

"Who's the other party you're mentioning?" Cole had demanded.

"I can't tell you now," Lawson had replied irritably. "He's helping to run this thing, but I'm bossing it."

"Maybe it's that bozo who calls himself Bond an' who's got you all buffaloed," Cole had ventured.

"He'd have been cracked off long ago if I hadn't kept everything quiet," had been Lawson's angry retort.

"Ah! Then . . . it's Farlin!"

Bond had found it necessary to leave after this to avoid being discovered by the night hawk watching the outlaws' horses.

Now, as he watched the outlaws dozing under the trees in the late afternoon sun, he began to scan the flowing plain to westward for sign of Dan Farlin. If Farlin decided that Gladys had eloped with Bond, the gambler might throw discretion to the winds in his rage and disappointment—which, though Bond did not actually know it, was exactly what the gambler had done.

In the last fading, purple glow of the twilight, Farlin came into sight, riding fast from the west. The rendezvous would soon be completed. Jim Bond carefully picked his way out of the breaks in the gathering shades of night, to sweep across the darkened plain and take up his station at the edge of town. With Cole gone, would Farlin and Lawson attempt the raid alone?

* * * * *

It lacked a few minutes of midnight when Jim Bond saw two riders streaking down from the north. Long before they drew opposite his secluded position in the shadows of the timber that grew along the little creek flowing down from Crazy Butte, he recognized Farlin and Lawson on their horses.

He let them thunder past, his eyes straining into the north, and shortly afterward caught sight of a dense, moving shadow. The outlaw band. So Lawson was bringing his band into town, after all. This was the first move in Lawson's double-cross—for

Bond knew that it was not Farlin's intention to allow more men at the actual scene of the raid than he thought he could, in dire emergency, handle alone.

As soon as Farlin and Lawson had passed and Bond had caught sight of the movement of the outlaw band, he slipped swiftly through the shadows on his way to town.

Rocky Point was dark and the streets deserted with only the yellow gleams of lamplight, which filtered through windows and doors of a few resorts, streaming across the sidewalks of the main street.

Farlin and Lawson rode in cautiously behind the bank. They had circled the town at a slow pace and come in through the trees. As they halted their walking horses, Farlin gave the signal to dismount. Then Farlin turned on the outlaw leader and spoke in a low voice: "You've got the stuff?" he said.

"I didn't bring along any peppermint candy to blow a safe with," was Lawson's gruff reply.

"Don't talk so loud," was the order in an undertone. "I'm going to let you into the bank. I've made a key that will work the back door. You know where the safe is, or I'll show you. It's an old-timer, but you'll have to do the business fast." The gambler's right hand twitched and his Derringer lay in his palm. "Listen, Ed, I'm going to keep you covered from now until we split . . . and we're going to split before we leave town."

Lawson snarled and started to move his gun hand. The look in Farlin's eyes stayed him.

"I've only got two slugs," said the gambler softly, "but they're both for you if you start anything. Choose your own time, Ed . . . or break clear afterward, as you see fit."

Lawson motioned viciously toward the rear door of the bank. "Go ahead," he snapped out.

"After you," said Farlin meaningfully.

Lawson strode forward with a muttered curse. He carried a small sack—the powder and tools for shattering the doors of the safe. Farlin followed, with the deadly Derringer snuggled in his right hand and the key to the door in his left. Clouds scuttled across the sky and the shadows danced, wavered, hesitated in the small open space behind the bank.

The key was turning in the lock when the thunder of flying hoofs awoke the sleeping town. The outlaws, a bit in advance of their leader's orders, were sweeping in to cover the retreat. At the last Lawson had shown his colors—he had been afraid to go through with the thing alone in town and leave his gang to ward off a posse outside of town. He had ordered them to come in.

Farlin leaped back from the door he was in the act of opening. He left the key sticking in the lock. At this moment a shadow drifted over his head, there was a gentle swish in the air, and a rope fell about his shoulders as his Derringer spit fire aimlessly in the night.

Lawson dropped the sack and whirled his back toward the door, his gun jumping into his hand. He thought he saw Farlin crawling away. In reality the gambler was being dragged by a rope in the hands of Jim Bond. In a trice Lawson saw the slim shadow and leaped toward Bond. Bond gave a mighty heave on the rope, jerking Farlin into the shadow of the trees, and stepped lightly toward Lawson.

By some queer shift of the wind, timed by some celestial arbiter, the clouds were swept away and the moonlight streamed into the space behind the bank. The pounding of horses' hoofs was in the air, shouts came from the street, and it seemed as if the whole town had been roused in the instant that Farlin's futile shots had broken on the still night air.

Lawson's eyes were flaming a deadly red as he confronted Bond.

"So you were goin' to horn in on this, single-handed!" he shot through his teeth. "Or maybe you framed it!" His words ended in a shout as horses began pouring into the restricted space.

"You were afraid to try it single-handed," Bond taunted. "And you were going to frame Farlin, you beginner!"

"So you are this Bovert!" Lawson exploded. "You came north to get Ed Lawson's card. Here it is!"

But Jim Bond's move was so lightning fast that his gun was flaming before Lawson could shoot. The big outlaw staggered and fell on his back almost under the hoofs of his own riders' horses. Bond leaped back into the shadow of the trees, drawing another weapon. He emptied both guns as he darted among the trees. Riderless horses reared and townsmen poured into the space behind the bank. The members of Lawson's outfit left their dead leader on the ground and raced away, those that were left.

Bond was holding Farlin by the arm, relieving him of the rope and speaking swiftly in his ear in an undertone. "The raid is over, you fool, and you're under cover. Do as I say, or . . . ."

Farlin didn't wait to hear the rest. He jerked himself free and swung at Bond with such force that he stumbled ahead several paces. The next moment the heavy barrel of one of Bond's guns crashed against his head and the world went inky black.

In the confusion and the futile chase of the surviving bandits, Jim Bond carried Farlin to the rear entrance of the hotel.

Chapter Twenty-Five

Porky's eyes were half closed when Sheriff Mills entered his room. The official had met the doctor on the way.

"He's sinking," the doctor had said. "I guess the excitement has been too much for him."

"Are you sure Lester didn't hit him?" the sheriff had asked.

"Never had a chance to fire," the doctor replied.

After this the official had looked steadily at the physician for some moments. "Now, Doc, give it to me square. How long is Porky going to last?"

"I don't know," returned the man of medicine. "I think he's bleeding internally."

"And that's not so good," the sheriff had observed.

Now, as the official stood staring at the wasted figure in the bed, he realized that his observation had been correct. He drew a chair close to the bed and sat down. Porky tried to move but merely groaned. His face was the color of ashes and his lips were blue.

The sheriff spoke in a low, vibrating voice: "I'm not going to ask you how you feel, Porky, because I can tell by the way you look. You're in a tight hole. You can tell me what you want to tell me, and that's all I'm asking of you. Take your time."

The sick man motioned toward the top drawer of the bureau and nodded faintly. Sheriff Mills crossed quickly to the bureau, and, when he opened the top drawer, he understood. He took out the bottle, poured some of its contents into a glass, added some water from a pitcher on the stand, raised Porky's head a little, and held the glass to his lips.

Porky drank the contents. His eyes widened a little and brightened under the stimulant. He coughed slightly and a pink froth bubbled on his lips. The sheriff waited and finally the sick man's words came fairly strong: "Gladys Farlin sent a note down to me addressed to Jim Bond. Bond had told me to get any message for him delivered through you." He paused while Sheriff Mills nodded in surprise. "Lester came in and found the note." Porky continued painfully. "I threw my gun on him an' told him to drop it. Instead he tore it open. Then I let him have it."

"Do you know what was in the note?" asked the sheriff.

"Yes, I read it and burned it up. It was to tell Bond that Lawson was back in town an' Dan was acting queer. I reckon you know that Lawson was dragging Dan into a job. That's all I've got to say. You must know all about it."

The sheriff shook his head. "I don't," he confessed, "but I'm doing a powerful lot of guessing."

A flush came into Porky's withered cheeks and he strove to raise himself.

"It's the Rocky Point bank!" he cried hoarsely as another fit of coughing seized him. Red blood stained his lips as he whispered: "Listen, Sheriff . . . Dan ain't to blame." The sheriff leaned over him to catch his next words. "I took . . . a chance on Bond being all right. If he is . . . give me credit . . . for . . . one good turn . . . before I pass out."

His frail frame shook with a violent paroxysm of coughing, and the blood spurted from his mouth. Sheriff Mills leaped to the door and called loudly for the clerk. When he turned back into the room, Porky Snyder lay still, his eyes wide in the fixed stare of death.

* * * * *

It was broad daylight when Dan Farlin regained consciousness. He didn't open his eyes at once, but lay still in bed, groping vaguely in his mind to piece together the events of the night before and the early morning. Gradually his memory of what had preceded the attempted bank robbery returned. He knew, of course, that Bond had roped him and later had shot Lawson down in a lightning gun play. He knew, too, that Bond had knocked him senseless with his gun and had carried him away from the scene when the space behind the bank was swarming with horses, and the town had suddenly become alive with excited, shouting men. He recalled dimly the figure of a woman at the head of the stairs when Bond had taken him into a building. He remembered vaguely voices about him and swallowing something out of a glass that must have been a sleeping potion, for the voices had faded and he had lapsed into oblivion.

When he opened his eyes, he saw at once that he was in a hotel room. The white curtains were fluttering about the window and bright sunlight was streaming across the carpet. His head throbbed with a dull pain and he raised a hand to find it was bandaged. Bond had seen that he had been taken care of, he realized with a frown. Why? The gambler smiled grimly. The reason, in his opinion, was plain. Bond had succeeded in luring Gladys away from Sunrise and had brought her to Rocky Point. He might even have married her! Farlin's jaw clamped shut. Bond had stumbled upon the bank job and probably had figured on finishing it himself. The arrival of the horsemen had nipped that scheme. Later Bond had kept what he knew to himself and had doubtless taken Gladys away. Farlin gave up further attempt at reasoning or conjecture because of the pain in his head. He closed his eyes until the door opened softly, and Jim Bond stepped in.

"Take it easy," said Bond as he closed the door and moved a chair to the side of the bed. He sat down and looked steadily at Farlin, shaking his head. "Get just as mad as you please, but I'll do the talking," he said in an impressive tone.

"One question," Farlin snapped. "Where's Gladys?"

"She's in Rocky Point in this very hotel. I told her just enough to persuade her to leave Sunrise and I brought her here safely. I've shot square with her and I'm in love with her whether you like it or not." He nodded convincingly. "You'll see her shortly. I didn't think it was any too safe for her in Sunrise and she trusted me."

Farlin's eyes were hard, but he was listening intently. He made no attempt to interrupt as Bond continued.

"I got wind of this bank business some time back, but I'm not going to tell you how. I decided to butt into this play to keep you from getting yourself in bad and double-crossed by Lawson in the bargain. Gladys was worried because she thought something was up and didn't want you to mix with Lawson. What I did, I did for her sake, and don't ever forget that."

The look in Farlin's eyes had changed to a gleam of keen interest. There was no mistaking the sincerity in Bond's tone, and his eyes showed that he was deeply in earnest.

"I had to give you that clout on the head last night to get you out of there quick. Those riders were Lawson's gang and I happen to know that you didn't expect them. It was just the start of Lawson's double-cross. I believe he intended to kill you right there at the bank and leave you for the sheriff to puzzle over."

Farlin asked for a glass of water, and drank it, nodding his thanks.

"All of the gang didn't get away," Bond continued. "Two of them are in jail, wounded. They've talked plenty and haven't had anything good to say for Lawson. They don't seem to understand just what your part in the play was, and it's just as well they don't. So far as I know, the sheriff and I are the only two outsiders who know about your connection with the affair."

"How much does the sheriff know?" Farlin asked quietly.

"You have me there," Bond replied. "He got in town about half an hour after the thing was over. He knows I brought you here and got the doctor for you, and he knows I put Lawson away. He knows Gladys and I left Sunrise together, and I think he believes you followed us here. That's the thing to tell him anyway. I didn't talk with him much and I didn't tell him anything. But he told me not to leave town, so he will be talking to me again. And he'll be in to see you. What he might have found out in Sunrise I don't know, either."

"Porky might have told him something," Farlin said dryly.

"Porky's dead," said Bond bluntly. "Bled to death inside, I heard. You're an older and smarter man than I am, Farlin, but, if I were you, I wouldn't say any more than I had to, to anybody. And don't blame Gladys for coming with me. I told her you were headed this way, too."

"Did you tell her why I was coming?" asked Farlin quickly.

"I gave her a pretty broad hint," replied Bond, "but you'll have to ask her any further questions." He held up a warning finger as a soft tapping was heard on the door, then he rose quickly, and nodded to Farlin.

"Come in," called Farlin.

It was Gladys Farlin who entered and in another moment her arms were about her father and she was kissing him.

"I'm so sorry, Daddy," she said in a voice that trembled. "But everything is going to be all right . . . I just know it is."

Bond had moved to the door. "I'll be back later," he said, smiling, and was out of the room before either of them could stop him.

"How'd you come to ride off with him?" Farlin asked the girl, stroking her hair.

"Because, Daddy, he knew what was going to happen here, although he didn't tell me in so many words. He said it was best to come and I . . . I trusted him. I knew when you told me that we were going to leave so soon that you planned to make a big stake quickly. Oh, I'm not blaming you a bit for wanting to do this. But I do blame Lawson. I won't say anything more about that because Lawson is gone. I never trusted him and I guess Jim Bond has told you how he planned to double-cross you. I wanted to help you, and Jim has helped us both."

"You call him by his first name, then?" her father asked in a low, queer voice.

"It isn't strange for people to call each other by their first names in this country, Daddy," she answered softly, pressing his hand.

"It's different in this case, Gladys. I suppose you know the kind of reputation this man has. Maybe he did do us a favor, but . . . well, I'm only thinking of you, dearie."

"Daddy, from what I've seen of Jim Bond, he could not be bad enough to be this man they call Bovert. And, even if he is . . . I . . . I don't care."

"Gladys!" her father exclaimed. "You don't know what you're saying. I can see he has a way with women, and I expect he's been telling you things."

"He told me he loved me," the girl said in a low voice, "and I believe him."

There was a long silence. Farlin was at a disadvantage, for regardless of who Bond really was, the fact remained that he had saved Farlin's life. And so far, he had played square.

After a time the gambler put the question he dreaded to ask: "How do you feel about him, Gladys?"

"Oh . . . I'm not sure."

Both welcomed the knock on the door at this moment. The visitor who responded to Farlin's invitation to enter proved to be Sheriff Mills.

The sheriff puckered his brows in a mock scowl as he looked from one to the other of them. "So you found your girl," he said to Farlin. Then, looking critically at Gladys: "She doesn't seem to be any the worse for riding from Sunrise to Rocky Point, and she had a good man with her."

"What do you know about him?" asked Farlin.

"I know he got rid of a bad one for me, meaning Lawson," said Mills with a frown, "and he sure did you a good turn. What's more, I'll bet the young lady will say he's played square with her."

"Maybe I'd better go," said Gladys.

"No, you better stay right here," drawled the sheriff. "I reckon you know as much about this business as I do, but there's one thing neither of you know and that is that we've got to give Porky Snyder credit for puncturing the schemes of Lester and Lawson."

"So he told Bond!" Farlin exclaimed, rising on an elbow. "I always thought that little runt knew more than he would own up to. And this fellow Bond isn't Bovert after all. He's the law!"

"No, Dan, he isn't the law in any way whatsoever. And I'm not saying whether he is Bovert or not. What he did . . . which was plenty . . . he did on his own hook without my knowledge. He sent a message to be delivered to me through Porky. So maybe he figured on seeing me and letting me in on the play. But I reckon he got side-tracked on the trail of Lawson and his gang."

"*Hm-m-m*," grunted Farlin. "You've just the same as told me that he is this gun terror. Then what was your idea in telling us to lay off of him?"

"Well, if he is what you think, I told you that to direct attention at him," drawled the sheriff. "And maybe he wasn't as bad as I thought, but I expected Lawson to get jealous and stage a gun play. I might have got rid of one of them, Lawson, say, or both. Lawson's day was done. Sunrise's day as a wild town was done. The law's come to Sunrise, Dan, and it's going to stay there. Sunrise is going to be a decent town and there's a bunch of settlers coming in this fall to supply it with decent trade of the right sort. With Lawson and his gang gone and Big Tom out of the way, the new order of things starts." He nodded gravely.

"And that puts me out of business," Farlin observed wryly.

"You needn't worry, Dan. You'd have quit anyway with this last play and I'm not blaming you, exactly, considering your state of mind, for taking the wild chance. Something will turn up for you, Dan. And now listen." The sheriff leaned forward and spoke in a low, even tone. "I knew a whole lot about this business just now, but I'm forgetting it as fast as you can think. You followed Gladys into town because you thought she had run away with this Bond.

You blundered into the bank play, and Bond happened along and helped you stop the robbery. Now don't make a fool out of me by telling any other story." Mills got to his feet and took up his hat.

"Why, Sheriff!" cried Gladys. "That's what I call giving Daddy one grand, square deal."

"You just do some forgetting yourself, young lady," said Mills, shaking a stern finger at her. "After all"—with a sly look at Farlin—"I'm just a sort of cow sheriff."

"And I'm taking that back," said Farlin as the official went out the door.

* * * * *

An hour later, Jim Bond sat across the desk from Sheriff Mills in the latter's private office. Mills was chewing an unlighted cigar as usual. Bond was eying him curiously. He had dropped in after he had made sure Mills had interviewed Dan Farlin.

"Well, let's have it," he said somewhat impatiently.

"I had a talk with Farlin and his girl," said the sheriff, removing his cigar and leaning forward in his chair. "I told Dan how he happened to be here. He followed you and the girl, and you took her out of Sunrise because you thought things were getting pretty hot there. Farlin blundered into the bank raid and you stumbled along and helped him out. Isn't that so?"

"It's so, if you say so," was Bond's answer.

"So near as I can now make out, that's what took place," said the sheriff dryly. He opened the top drawer of his desk and took out an envelope. "I've got some papers here," he said casually, "and a photograph, although it isn't a very good one." He looked at Bond, whose eyes had narrowed slightly. "Fact is," he went on, "this picture is so bad I can't make anything out of it at all. Why, it might even be you, the way it looks."

"Just a snapshot, I suppose," Bond ventured, keeping his steady gaze on the sheriff. There was a suggestion of a puzzled frown on his face.

"Yes . . . just a snapshot of a man on a horse," said Mills. "Anyway, I have enough to look after here in my own territory without listening and bothering with what some outfit down south thinks about somebody or something."

Bond started as the sheriff deliberately tore papers, photograph, and envelope in half, and then tore the halves into small pieces. He opened the door of the cold stove and tossed in the fragments. Then he dropped in a lighted match. "That's the way I get rid of waste paper," he explained. "What do you figure on doing, Bond?"

The youth roused himself. "I . . . I hadn't made any plans," he stammered. "You're sure you know what you just did, Sheriff?"

"I'm not so old that I don't usually know what I'm doing, young man," said Mills coldly. "Now, about the girl. You think pretty well of Gladys Farlin, do you not?"

"Oh, well enough," Bond answered shortly.

"She's a nice girl," the sheriff went on in his even voice. "Too nice to play any tricks on." He gave Bond a sharp look, then held up a hand as Bond started to speak. "Never mind. There are going to be some opportunities out Sunrise way for a young fellow who has a little money, some brains, and isn't afraid to work. A piece of land out there could be made into a good-paying proposition, and that country out there is going to be sweet to live in from now on."

Bond brightened. "I haven't any fault to find with this country, Sheriff," he said with a confidential nod.

"Like other spots in the West, this is going to be a great wheat section," Mills observed. "But there'll always be room for cattle. Maybe not so many, but better stock. It wouldn't surprise me if Dan Farlin decided to stay in these parts. I know he'd stay if Gladys decided that she wanted to stay."

Bond was smiling very broadly. "Sheriff, you're a pretty smooth article." He laughed. "Wouldn't surprise me if you got just about anything you wanted."

"Well, I don't want much. I like to see people happy and contented, and I want to see this country come into its own with the right kind of people living in it. John Duggan, our banker, is a pretty good hand at giving advice to a young fellow who wants to get a start." He lifted his brows slightly.

Bond laughed outright in delight. "I get you, Sheriff. I'll be having a little talk with Mister Duggan."

"Not a bad idea," said Mills, looking at his watch. "Well, I expect by this time the doc has looked Dan over and maybe Duggan has dropped in to see him. Suppose we drift up that way."

"Before we go, Sheriff, I'd like to ask you a question," said Bond as they rose. "Why did you give 'em notice up in Sunrise to lay off this Bovert if he came along?"

"Maybe I wanted to see him, for one thing," replied the sheriff. "Maybe I intended to take him in before he could start more trouble than I had already. Maybe I wanted to see if he could get that crowd all tangled up and fighting with him and themselves and save me a lot of trouble by letting Sunrise clean up by itself." He smiled faintly. "What made you stop here, Bond?"

"Me? Why I didn't intend to stop here, Sheriff, I was on my way north. Then I met Gladys and found out something was up, and I stayed to play it out because . . . well, I liked her father, too."

"You mean you stayed to help him on *her* account, young man," said the sheriff sternly. "When I saw the way things were going, I sat back and looked on. You needn't take all the credit to yourself. Now, let's go."

Several persons were in Farlin's room at the hotel when Bond and Mills arrived. Farlin was up and dressed, save for his coat. The breakfast dishes still remained on a side table. Gladys was there, looking flushed and happy. George Reed, the amiable proprietor of the hotel, was present, and the round, genial face of the banker, John Duggan, beamed upon the assemblage.

"I was just thanking Dan, here, for helping to stop that no-good Lawson's deviltry, Sheriff," John Duggan boomed. "And there was something that outlaw didn't know." The banker chuckled and winked at the official. "He didn't know about that secret vault I had put in under the old one. He'd have had some trouble getting into that strong box, eh, Mills?"

"You shouldn't be telling the bank's secrets." Mills frowned.

"Well, it's my bank," Duggan said, laughing. "Of course I'm responsible to my directors," he added hastily, clearing his throat. "I was going to talk a bit with Dan, here, about his future. He's done a service that . . ."

"I'm not going to take any more credit for something I didn't do!" Farlin broke in loudly, slapping the table with an open palm.

"Dan Farlin, you shut up!" thundered the sheriff. "And you just listen to what John has to say."

"That's the ticket," said Duggan. "Now you've got your orders from headquarters. It's like this. Sunrise is going to boom. The days of making a living in this country by gambling are about over. So we won't think of you as a gambler any more, Dan. You have good business possibilities. You know men . . . which is important. And you know how to handle money outside of the slot in a gaming table. I'm going to fix up that ranch proposition of yours in Texas so you won't lose too much. What you need is two or three months' technical experience, we'll call it, in our bank here. Then, late this fall, I'm going to put in a branch up at Sunrise and put you in charge of it." The banker's big, friendly face glowed.

"Me?" Farlin gasped. "Me . . . a banker?" He laughed shortly. "I'd do better to buy out the Red Arrow and run it for a living."

"Some of Lester's relatives are going to look after that," said Duggan. "You'll do better to take up my proposition and you'll sort of dress up my bank."

"I think," drawled the sheriff, "that the matter is settled. Anyway, you'll be close enough to keep an eye on him, John, and help him out when he needs it. And I suppose he'll have a clerk or two to do the heavy work. He might even take some stock in it. Have you thought of that, John?"

"I've already decided how much he'll take," boomed Duggan.

Chapter Twenty-Six

Spring was blossoming into summer. It was evening and a cooling breeze was laving Sunrise in its magic setting of green. Red and golden banners of glory streamed in the western sky. Dan Farlin, straight, handsome, and elegant, stood on the little front porch of his cabin, looking down at the figures of a tall youth and a girl strolling on the grassy trail leading to town—the new town of Sunrise. Dan was up for over Sunday from the bank at Rocky Point.

"Yes, I've got a place," Jim Bond was telling Gladys Farlin. "Only four miles west of town. A hundred and sixty acres of homestead and I'm buying a piece of grazing land that adjoins it on time. We can have a little home of our own, Gladys. Tell me, don't you think it's time you answered my question?"

"Don't you think there's something you should tell me before . . . I answer, Jim?" she said in a low voice.

"I know." He nodded, taking her hands as they paused in the trail. "I was Bovert, sweetheart, but now I'm what I was in the first place. Just Jim Bond. And I owe it to you. Now you can answer, girlie, if you still trust me."

The girl looked up at him out of shining eyes. "I still trust you, Jim," she said softly. "I have to trust you because . . . because I love you." Jim Bond barely heard the last words before he took her in his arms.

"Then that's your answer," he said in a thrilling voice.

"Yes," she whispered as their lips met.

"And that's that," said Dan Farlin to himself as he turned back into the cabin. "I might have known it. Well, I guess I'll have to be satisfied."

"Was you speaking to me, Mister Dan?" asked the house-keeper as he entered the living room.

Dan Farlin roused himself at the unexpected voice. "Yes"— he smiled—"if you were quick enough to catch it."

He lit a cigarette and sat down on the divan to await the two young people who were strolling hand in hand up the path. He had an idea that they had something to tell him.

And he was right.

THE END

About the Author

Robert J. Horton was born in Coudersport, Pennsylvania in 1889. As a very young man he traveled extensively in the American West, working for newspapers. For several years he was sports editor for the Great Falls *Tribune* in Great Falls, Montana. He began writing Western fiction for Munsey's *All-Story Weekly* magazine before becoming a regular contributor to Street & Smith's *Western Story Magazine*. By the mid-1920s Horton was one of three authors to whom Street & Smith paid 5¢ a word—the other two being Frederick Faust, perhaps better known as Max Brand, and Robert Ormond Case. Some of Horton's serials for Street & Smith's *Western Story Magazine* were subsequently brought out as books by Chelsea House, Street & Smith's book publishing company. Although all of Horton's stories appeared under his byline in the magazine, for their book editions Chelsea House published them either as by Robert J. Horton or by James Roberts. Sometimes, as was the case with *Rovin' Redden* (Chelsea House, 1925) by James Roberts, a book would consist of three short novels that were editorially joined to form a "novel" and seriously abridged in the process. Other times the stories were magazine serials, also abridged to appear in book form, such as *Unwelcome Settlers* (Chelsea House, 1925) by James Roberts or *The Prairie Shrine* (Chelsea House, 1924) by Robert J. Horton. It may be obvious that Chelsea House, doing a number of books a year by the same author, thought it a prudent marketing strategy to give the author more than one name. Horton's Western stories are concerned most of all with character, and it is the characters that drive the plots rather than the other way around. Attended by his personal physician, he died of bronchial pneumonia in his Manhattan hotel room in 1934 at the relatively early age of forty-four. Several of his novels, after Street & Smith abandoned Chelsea House, were published only in British editions, and Robert J. Horton was not to appear at all in paperback books until quite recently. *Rainbow Range* will be his next **Five Star Western.**